Fit to Kill

A Novel
by Donnie Ray Whetstone

Published by StoneCart Books,
    A division of StoneCart Enterprises,
    P.O.Box 249, Littlerock, WA 98556

Cover design by Rhonda M. Huynh
Book design by Diane C. Whetstone
Photograph of Donnie Whetstone by Mark Mason
Edited by Tracy Papachristodoulou

ISBN: 1470107740
ISBN-13: 978-1470107741

Published in the United States of America

To my grandmother, Pricilla Cole, rest in peace Grandma

To my parents, Otis and Ophelia Whetstone

To my siblings, Alvin and Kenneth Whetstone and
Rausilune Gillespie

To my kids, Troy, Tia and Torian Whetstone, David Salang
and Mary Lou Sandler

To my wife and inspiration, Diane Whetstone

Table of Contents

CHAPTER 1

La Flore

The sun creeps over the horizon, its beams piercing the cloudless summer sky, waking the city of La Flore. This sprawling scenic city of four hundred thousand has had a good year. Forbes magazine ranks it fifteenth on its list of best places to live. Better Health magazine has La Flore top five on its list of healthiest cities. Two of its five high school sports teams, the La Flore Bears football team and the Woodland Hills Pirates women's basketball team, won this year's 5A State Championships.

Its towering skyline stands majestically in the morning sun while the hustle and bustle of downtown life begins its daily cycle. Shops ranging from Mom & Pops to those found at the ever-popular Mega Mall, open their blinds to invite the new day. Humble homes and apartment complexes on La Flore's Lower East Side along with the lavish homes and condominiums of Woodland Hills, nestle lazily in the morning as equals. Gilder Park, the most popular of the city's scenic parks is dotted with early morning fitness buffs jogging, cycling and power walking its manicured trails and roadways. They are seen in fitness clubs, gyms and private training studios scattered throughout the city. Being listed in the top five healthiest cities by Better Health magazine is well deserved by its sheer number of fitness facilities. Well-known gyms like 24 Hour Fitness and Gold's Gym exist along with local generic brands like the hardcore Iron Man's Gym, and the Roman Health Club. Those seeking plush surroundings with every amenity frequent the lavish Woodland Hills Athletic Club where an annual membership for a single La Florian will set them back three thousand dollars, sales tax not included.

Other popular fitness venues for La Florians are private personal training studios. They provide personal service and fitness disciplines that their larger counterparts cannot match. Pilates by Monique, Kevin's MMA and Chad's Pro Fitness are just a few among the hefty list of private training studios La Florians flock to.

These trainers are as unique as their studios. While trainers at a typical gym vary in skill level, they are the industry's foot soldiers, while the owners of La Flore's private studios are the fitness elite with the experience, skill level, business savvy and confidence to customize, personalize and oversee workouts that demand the top dollar La Florians willingly dish out.

One such studio is located on the La Flore's west side. It is in a lush secluded area where scores of private offices and a few tall buildings dot the landscape. Of modest size, the studio sits next to Baker Brothers BMW Auto Sales. A simple but immaculate sign mounted next to the entrance with red block letters against a white background reads, "Fit Now Private Personal Training." Inside is a small waiting area with a front desk that is unattended since Becky, the receptionist, is not due to arrive until nine a.m. The cardio room houses a treadmill, an elliptical machine and a stationary bike with each piece parked in front of its own wall-mounted flat screen TV.

An office, a single coed bathroom and change room separates the plush cardio room from the training floor. Waist level mirrors run along three of the four walls of the enclosed main training floor making the room look much larger than its nine hundred square feet. The training floor has an array of free weights and machines. An abused heavy bag hangs at the far end of the room. Speakers are mounted on all corners of the training floor and provide a perk that sets La Flore's private studios apart from their counterparts; theater grade surround sound to a client's favorite satellite music station or CD.

Speakers transform the music from Aerosmith's Greatest Hits into a live concert with front row seats. It is Wanda Brooke's second consecutive month playing the CD. She assaults the plate loaded leg press for a grueling fifteen reps while the song "Just Press Play" and the firm barking of her trainer give her inspiration. She is ten minutes into her thirty-minute gauntlet, otherwise known as leg day. Anyone who knows her would not be surprised that leg day, loathed by many clients, is her favorite. Wanda had been a highly driven athlete all through high school and college. Family life plus a thriving career as a drug rep has not slowed down the trim well-toned thirty-eight year old brunette.

"Is it time for that surprise you promised?" she asks, between heavy breaths while laying semi limp on the leg press machine.

"No, not yet…but we're getting there," her trainer responds.

The workout continues and the duo are now in full throttle with the trainer in his zone and Wanda pounding out one demanding set after another.

"Give me more Wanda! C'mon! I want more!"

The tone of the trainer's voice, along with the heavy breathing and grunting from his client, could easily mislead a person not privy to what was happening, into believing that trainer and client were engaged in unbridled sex, rather than a training session.

Later, Wanda lays sprawled out, face up on the training floor drenched in sweat with arms and legs stretched out; a common posture for her after a leg workout.

"That was a great one. I take it we're at that time now," she says, exhausted. The endorphin rush makes her oblivious to her surroundings. The trainer observes his client with an unwavering stare from a bench he is straddling.

"Yes, Wanda, I believe it is."

"So, what is it you're going to do that you promised me?"

"Don't worry; you're going to love it. Close your eyes." he says with an air of confidence. Wanda, feeling euphoric, closes her eyes, exposing near perfect teeth, smiling in eager anticipation. After a time of darkness and silence, "Are you ready?" she hears the trainer ask. Wanda responds, still in her euphoric state, "Yes, I'm ready."

Overtaken by curiosity, she opens her eyes. A surge of adrenaline instantly kills her endorphin high. Her mind cannot relay the input to her muscles fast enough to avoid the fifty-pound dumbbell dropped lengthwise from a height of six feet, now hurling towards her face. The heavy metal projectile slams dead center on its intended target, delivering a crushing blow followed by a loud distinct crunch, as if someone had stepped on a large insect. The dumbbell, now stained with blood, rolls harmlessly to a stop leaving a gruesome trail. Wanda's body spasms while expelling urine and feces. Her head, once that of an attractive woman, now resembles a broken vase with its parts and contents scattered about the training floor. The trainer casually kneels over his victim to examine the carnage left by the deadly collision. The smell of fresh blood, exposed flesh and brain matter is pungent, filling his nostrils. He kneels and his gaze traverses the body from toe to what was once his client's head. The trainer stares keenly at the fragmented mass. He smiles after a moment, and then confidently says, "See Wanda, I knew you'd love it."

CHAPTER 2

Sheridan Park

The morning dew covering the woody terrain of Sheridan Park located on La Flore's north side gradually dissipates as a crime scene slowly unfolds. Bands of yellow tape begin to form a thirty square foot perimeter around a lifeless body. A middle-aged couple and their golden retriever discover the body of a woman lying within a cluster of trees and brush while embarking on their ritual morning walk. The husband embraces and consoles his wife. Her blank stare and ashen skin tells him she is in a state of shock from the grisly discovery. An officer, observing the severity of the wife's condition, calls for an ambulance to attend her as he waits for an opportunity to interview the husband.

Later that morning, the crime scene is abuzz with activity as additional squad cars, an ambulance and a CSI van arrive. Many park patrons are curious about the ominous activity and abandon their morning doings to become spectators. Although La Flore is not immune to homicides, they do not happen very often. Mayor Myron Hondo Saks, affectionately referred to as Hondo, along with La Flore's "Top Cop" Vince Nirez, proudly boast the city's violent crime rate is among the lowest in the nation. They have vowed it would remain that way on their watch.

Two unmarked cars arrive, trailed by a news van. Emerging from the first car is Detective Calvin McVey, a thirty eight year old, six foot former Marine MP Captain with a fresh crew cut and beach boy looks. He holds the distinction of serving five consecutive tours of duty in Iraq at the height of its bloody insurgency. Hunting elusive killers and seeing a degree of bloodshed that would severely damage the psyche of most, more than makes up for his mere three years of experience as a detective. He stands and waits by his vehicle. With blue eyes, deep set and piercing, he observes the controlled chaos ten yards in front of him.

The second detective joins McVey. Detective Bob Cummins is a La Flore native and former standout quarterback for the La Flore Bears back in the day. He received the MVP award in their second State Championship win when his team miraculously demolished an undefeated opponent that was the unanimous favorite. A full ride scholarship to Boise State and a high probability of playing football on Sundays ended tragically with a career ending knee injury. As a result, he abandoned his lifelong dream of fortune and fame to pursue law enforcement. Cummins, now forty-two, a fifteen-year veteran detective and a full inch taller than McVey, looks around, reminiscing. This is where his team had their private post state victory party. It is here where the hottest members of the cheerleading squad fulfilled their promised rewards for the miracle victory.

"Where's Tanner?" Cummins asks scanning the area.

"I don't know," McVey replies. "Personally speaking, I don't care," he says sarcastically under his breath.

The two walk casually toward the crime scene. Passing them is a news team consisting of a camera operator and reporter Carol Chase of KAPO 7 News. They scurry to the scene to set up a live report. When the two detectives approach the crime scene, an officer meets them and seeing their detective badges, escorts them inside the perimeter.

Soon afterward, a third unmarked car appears and parks a few feet behind the news van. Inside, Detective Tara Tanner sits for a moment gazing at both of her hands in a firm grip on top of the steering wheel. She fixes her dark eyes on the crime scene that is finally starting to lose its frenzy. After a long sigh, she emerges from her car. Tara's eyes stay glued on the crime scene. Her five foot eight athletic frame strolls past the vehicles of Cummins and McVey.

It's been a long time since we've had one of these, she thinks.

Although the forty year-old detective grew up on La Flore's Lower East Side, she is not a native. Her family, a rather dysfunctional one, moved to La Flore from Hueytown, Alabama, a small town just outside of Birmingham, when she was eleven years old. Her father, who she loved dearly, was a functional alcoholic with a rapacious thirst for Seagram 7. Her mother, who she blamed for his affliction, was a philanderer with a rapacious appetite for younger men. Nearly thirty years as a La Florian has all but eroded the heavy southern drawl she was often teased for as a teenager; but enough remains to spark curiosity in listeners during a conversation. At twenty, Tara attended La Flore's City University as a single mom working two jobs after going through a bitter divorce after only eight months of marriage. Although she prides herself as having a keen nose for bad souls, which greatly influenced her decision to become a detective, it often failed her in matters of the heart. Tara went through a string of abusive relationships throughout her twenties. She met her present husband, Dale, when she was twenty-nine and they married a year later. A nine-year veteran, Tara's tenure as a detective in La Flore is a mixed bag. Her keen intuition has been instrumental in putting away some of La Flore's most notorious criminals. She has earned several commendations including the city's prestigious Medal of Valor award presented by Mayor Hondo Saks himself for solving La Flore's biggest criminal case in recent times.

Tara was grief stricken upon the death of her father, affecting her instincts. She was the lead detective in a controversial case shortly after her father died. The infamous Sexton case resulted in the deaths of two people, one, a four-year-old child. As a result, Tara felt she had lost her intuitive touch and wanted to resign, even though an extensive inquiry cleared her of any wrongdoing. Tara's decision whether or not to resign became a highly controversial topic within Division. Her decision to remain a detective was encouraged by her long time boss Commander Robert Johnson, a six foot seven former NBA player with the Portland Trailblazers.

Arriving at the tape of the crime scene, Tara encounters the same officer who met McVey and Cummins and upon flashing her glaring gold ornamental shield of La Flore's Detective Division, is escorted inside the perimeter. She dons a pair of surgical gloves she had retrieved from her trouser pocket. She immediately sees Cummins and McVey, and then fixes her eyes on the gruesome sight at their feet, a female body with virtually no head.

"This is some piece of work." Cummins says as Tara approaches within earshot of the two detectives.

"Yeah, to say the least," McVey adds.

"Hey Tanner, glad to see you could make it this fine morning," Cummins exclaims in a lighthearted tone.

Tara joins her colleagues and intensely scans over the victim.

"So, give us an expert opinion, Sherlock," Cummins says.

His obnoxious humor draws a cynical grin from McVey that she catches. Not in the mood to deal with him, she lets it go.

"Well, it's not a decapitation, her neck is not severed," Tara says.

"You're right," a voice intrudes.

The voice comes from the CSI leader and acquaintance of the three detectives, Nolan Sumner.

"From a preliminary standpoint, the victim died of blunt force trauma to the face and a violent one at that."

"So simply put, she got her brains bashed in," Tara concludes.

"I'm afraid so," Sumner replies.

"We'll confirm the ID once we're at the lab, but judging by the tattoo on her left ankle, I'm positive the victim is our missing person."

The small tattoo depicts a pair of doves in flight over a banner. Engraved on the banner are the letters "BFFL" meaning "Best Friends for Life". The tattoo is identical to the one worn on the left ankle of Sophia Palomar, who reported her missing. Sophia has been the victim's best friend since grade school. She asserts they both got the tattoos together, as sophomores in college, to signify their undying friendship. The missing person, Terri Gibson, is a thirty-six year old assistant manager at one of La Flore's high-end clothing stores. Terri, along with Sophia, coach the Lady Hawks, a girls league soccer team.

"I can't imagine anyone having enough of a beef with this woman to do this," Detective Cummins says.

"Apparently somebody did," Tara responds, looking upon the carnage spread out before her. She looks around to observe the picturesque splendor of Sheridan Park with La Flore's scenic skyline standing in the background. Then, a sense of foreboding snatches her back to reality when she gazes once more upon the unfortunate victim.

She does not get a chance for a word or thought as to the wayward soul responsible for such an unspeakable act before a stern voice speaks for her.

Detective McVey boldly proclaims, "Or... whoever did this, is just one evil son of a bitch."

CHAPTER 3

Careful What You Wish For

Thelma Carson epitomizes what an unwavering commitment to training, a healthy lifestyle, great genetics and a little help from a gifted cosmetic surgeon, who happens to be a close friend, can accomplish. At sixty-one, her five foot six inch frame can easily rival that of an exceptional looking woman in her forties. With silky brown hair, an alluring smile and her trademark green eyes, many local women's magazines praise Thelma. Their accolades give her a great deal of happiness and sense of accomplishment, but it is her ability to spawn the arousal of men less than half her age, that pleases her the most.

She and her husband Bob own a number of businesses inside and outside of La Flore. They are a part of La Flore's elite, residing in Woodland Hill's most exclusive area. Raising three kids, building a small empire and occasionally, running across a perfume scented phone number or a hotel stub in her husband's coat pocket, have taken their toll on her. At times, when she's feeling down, Thelma ponders the notion, with all of the accoutrements she and her husband have accumulated over the years that they have actually lost far more than they have gained. She is a far cry from feeling that way this evening. Bob is out of town for another week and the staff is gone for the day. The sounds emanating from her bedroom are unmistakable.

Thelma's pelvis works her partner's tool as she moans uncontrollably.

"Now?" he asks with remarkable composure.

Thelma does all she can to convey to him what she wants.

"Ok then."

Her partner slows his rhythm, causing her head to thrash gently.

"I want you to hold it," he says calmly. "I want you to hold it longer than last time."

She cannot speak and is fighting a losing battle of containing a category five orgasm.

"Just a little longer; you can do it," he says encouragingly.

Her head now thrashes violently as the attempt to contain herself becomes unbearable.

"See, Thelma, you did it. Now let it go."

Her cry echoes throughout the enormous house. She succumbs to the massive release of dopamine and endorphins that engulf her. After her release, her body goes limp, overwhelmed by passion and exhaustion.

Later that evening, she lies face down on the sturdy king size oak bed. A white satin sheet covers her from the waist down. With her eyes closed, she basks in the afterglow of her intense experience.

"I don't know what's better, your training sessions or your sex," she says.

Thelma's eyes open, and she finds herself lying in bed alone. Looking around, she sees her partner, standing nude at the foot of the bed, leaning on the heavy footboard with muscular arms outstretched and unreadable eyes focused on her.

"How long have you been there?" she asks.

"Just a few minutes," he replies.

She reaches out her hand and he capitulates. He lies in bed with her and she rests her head on his well-developed chest. There are no illusions in her mind that this will go beyond sex; he has made it quite clear. Though she has more than one stud in her stable, Thelma feels the hundred and fifty thousand dollars she invested in his training studio is well worth the physical fulfillment he gives her.

Silence fills the room as they lay together. Soon, a question that has been eating at her breaks the quiet.

"Did you, you know, cum this time?" she asks, trying not to be offensive.

Her partner answers her question with stoic silence.

"I'm not saying you have any hang ups, but other guys can barely last five minutes with me. I just want to know if I'm pleasing you as much as you're…"

"Do you want me to?" he asks, in an abrupt tone. "I will, if that's what you want."

Thelma's head has stopped spinning but her body has not fully recovered. Still, the opportunity to satisfy the only partner to take her to such sexual heights is too strong to turn down. What she does not realize with this partner, is there are times, to be careful what you wish for.

"Yeah, it's what I want," she replies.

It does not take long for his member to respond, to her surprise, fuller and harder for what awaits.

"Come," he gestures softly, holding out his hand, wearing a placid face.

He gently positions her on all fours in the middle of the bed, facing the headboard. From behind her, he slowly runs his hands along her back and upon reaching her shoulders, presses her gently onto a pillow, with her hips vaulted and exposed.

Thelma becomes aroused again, A little to her surprise, as she is still spent from their last bout. Her breath becomes heavy as her heartbeat quickens. The two moan as they join together. He penetrates her deeply; gently working his hardness while strong hands caress her back. She can tell her partner is far more aroused than earlier.

"Is this what you want?" she asks in a seductive tone.

"Yes. This is what I want."

"I want you to cum for me," she says, starting to lose herself.

In a voice not nearly as controlled as the previous session, he replies, "I will, real soon."

He places a hand behind her head and presses it firmly into the pillow. His movement gradually becomes intense, then painful, finally, brutal. Thelma emits agonizing screams but her face lodged in the pillow muffles them. More ominously, she soon realizes it also inhibits her ability to breath.

Thelma tries to lift her face away from the pillow. She meets stiff resistance from her partner's talon-like grip. White satin sheets begin to stain with blood as she is mercilessly assailed with violent thrusts. Out of instinct, she reaches behind her head trying to pry away the hand locked on the back of her head to no avail. She begins flailing her arms frantically in a final attempt for precious oxygen.

"I'm almost there," says a voice that is now impassioned.

Her flailing arms soon go limp, then still. As life leaves her body, a deafening scream echoes throughout the house. In a single powerful contraction, a massive load of semen floods what is now a bloody grotesque wound. Exhausted, he gently lies on top of Thelma's lifeless body. He is breathing and sweating as if he has just finished an hour of cardio at top speed. Thelma's head remains lodged in the pillow as his breathing soon slows and returns to normal. He looks down upon what is now a lifeless corpse.

"My...you are a sadistic one," he says aloud, referring to himself. He gently turns her head to one side, pushing back her hair to expose an ear. Kissing her softly along the neck, he reaches her ear and calmly whispers,

"See Thelma...I knew you could make me do it. Was it as good for you as it was for me?"

CHAPTER 4

Witnessing History

The investigation of Terri Gibson's murder is only two weeks underway and sadly already starting to look like a random homicide.

"There is a killer in La Flore, to say the least," Tara's mind concludes. "The person that brutally ended Terri Gibson's life is probably watching TV, reading a book or enjoying a hot cup of coffee right now. They're doing all the things Terri Gibson no longer can. This cannot and will not go unpunished."

Curiosity grips Tara as she drives to La Flore's Central Precinct thirty minutes early, avoiding much of the morning traffic. The Central Precinct is one of four located throughout the city. It is by far the largest and serves as LFPD's headquarters. The body of a woman found late last night on La Flore's south side, is at the Forensics and Pathology Division. Tara arrives at the large gated compound. Parking, she approaches the three story main building and goes to a side entrance. She opens a large metal door and enters the building. A long hallway and two flights of stairs later, she arrives at the precinct's Pathology Division. Agent Nolan Sumner is in his office at his desk, thumbing through a stack of papers. Walking past the open doorway, Tara sees the agent, stops mid stride, and enters.

"Agent Sumner," Tara says, stepping in gingerly.

"Detective Tanner," the agent replies, "Come in." He gestures her to a seat. "Can I offer you some coffee?"

"No, no thanks," she answers, sitting down on a well-used armchair.

The forty-four year old pathologist has been at Division for fourteen years. He has a plain face with a thick head of salt and pepper hair and a closely cropped beard to match. His responsibilities as head of LFPD's Pathology Division leave him little time for exercise. Tara notices by the increased fullness of his face since their last meeting, and thinks that her close associate could stand to lose a few pounds from his five foot nine inch frame.

Tara feels he senses her eagerness to know about the victim in his examination room.

"Well, we just cleaned her up for a positive ID this morning. A family member should be here shortly."

A team member interrupts, "Boss…He's here…The husband."

"Proceed," Agent Sumner says along with a nod of his head.

Tara and Agent Sumner watch the team member and the victim's husband walk past the office doorway. A tall, husky man, Marcus Vogel moves like a death row inmate taking his final walk to the death chamber. Silence fills the office for what seems like an eternity as detective and agent brace themselves. The memory of Sophia's heart wrenching ordeal, the day she learned her lifelong friend was the Sheridan Park victim is still fresh on Tara's mind. She recalls thinking no one should ever experience what Sophia had to go through when:

"No, no. God no! Who would do this to my baby; who would do this?" Marcus immediately succumbs to gut wrenching sobs. Tara and the agent remain silent. Weakened with grief, Marcus is escorted away by two team members. Agent Sumner has an empty look on his face as he stares at his desk. In a solemn tone, the agent speaks.

"I've been in this business nearly twenty years, and despite all that I've seen, I can never get used to that; probably never will." He looks at Tara, "Shall we proceed, Detective?"

"By all means," she replies.

The two head towards the examination room. Upon entering, the intense energy released by the husband assails Tara. She cast her eyes on the metal table where the body lay, covered by a thin blue sheet.

"Who found her?" she asks.

"The night road crew found her off of Old Highway 77."

Standing over the examination table, the agent carefully folds back the sheet, exposing the victim's head and shoulders.

"She's been identified as Kelly Vogel, forty-four, mother of three, and I have a strong hunch, she was happily married."

"She's very pretty," Tara says, observing the deceased's face.

"She's a very popular figures competitor who recently earned her professional status, and you will soon see why. One of the road crew recognized her; that's how we got the initial I.D. She did some personal training on the side to fund her competing. She really didn't need to. Her husband runs a successful catering business."

"What's the cause of death?" Tara asks.

"Suffocation by smothering. The crewmen found her nude, faced-down. My team swept the area but couldn't find any clothing."

"Was there a sexual assault?"

The look Tara's colleague gives her answers her question. He gingerly pulls back the sheet. She is amazed at the magnificent body of the deceased, validating the agent's prediction. More so, she is appalled at the gaping obscenity that was once her vulva.

"Any ideas what caused this?"

"Well...not even a well endowed porn star could cause this type of damage," he replies, as if an expert on the subject. The comment produces a puzzled scowl on

Tara's face, knowing her colleague's virtuous demeanor. She shakes off his peculiar remark.

"The evidence tells me it was a large blunt instrument of some sort, large enough and used forcefully enough to do this type of damage. Judging by the lining of the vagina, it was also very abrasive," the agent says.

Detective McVey joins Tara and the agent. "So, I assume we have a positive I.D.," McVey says.

"Yeah, the husband identified the body," Sumner respond.

"I heard all about it. Is he going to be ok?" McVey asks.

"Let's hope so," Tara interjects.

McVey gives her a look bordering on contempt and total disgust.

Tara, emotionally charged from the husband's outburst and remembering the detective's expression at Sheridan Park, sees the look and this time, doesn't let it go.

"Detective McVey ... I don't know what your beef is with me, and at this point, I don't give a rat's ass. I'm not going to continue to take this shit from you simply because you don't have the balls to man up and spit it out!"

"Whoa, whoa, whoa…settle down, Detective," Agent Sumner says in an inflated tone.

McVey stands with both hands on his waist with piercing blue eyes focused on her like a drill sergeant about to pounce on a lowly private.

This has no effect as Tara stares back with dark defiant eyes, refusing to back down.

After a moment, "I've seen enough here," McVey says.

"Agent Sumner," he says dismissing himself, then briefly looking at Tara before walking away.

"What was that all about?" Sumner asks.

"Your guess is as good as mine," she replies, reeling from the altercation.

"Where was I?" the agent rambles, trying to collect his thoughts. "Oh yes, we did find semen at the scene but oddly, it wasn't present inside any of the body cavities. We're running tests to see what comes up."

"The question is how could someone do this?" the agent asks.

Tara, now recovered from her dispute with McVey, weighs in.

"Agent Sumner, someone did this because they're just one evil son of a bitch," she says, ironically paraphrasing McVey.

They look at each other and Agent Sumner immediately knows what she is insinuating.

"I wasn't sure until I saw that," she says, having a flash of genius. "That wound is more than just a wound, it's a signature. The same signature we saw at Sheridan Park."

Tara gazes upon the victim and speaks softly as if she expects an answer.

"Terri Gibson's murder was not just a random homicide; you saw her killer too, didn't you, Mrs. Vogel?" She faces the agent. "We're witnessing history here," she says with certainty, and remorse. The nodding of the agent's head tells Tara he sees the validity in her argument.

"Agent Sumner, I'm afraid our great city has its first serial killer."

CHAPTER 5

A Wall or a Mirror?

Dusk settles upon the city as Tara drives to her suburban home located on La Flore's south side. Her mind is in recap mode, replaying the stirring scene at Pathology and the emotional interviews with Kelly Vogel's clients and friends.

A serial killer is in La Flore. For once, I hope I'm wrong…but I don't think I am.

Despite her confidence, Tara senses her argument will meet resistance by some in Division, who two years since the Sexton case, still have little confidence in her.

It's a bit premature, other than the shocking wounds there is no solid MO, she asserts, playing devil's advocate with herself. *All I've really got is my gut…I just feel it.*

There was a time when Tara's gut would have been more than sufficient to eliminate any doubt in her mind, along with the unwavering support of the entire division.

Later, she turns onto Follett Drive and cruises the windy roadway through the well-kept upper middle class neighborhood and approaches a cul-de-sac, veers to the right and enters the driveway of a two-storey adobe-style house. Tara enters the quiet, cozy home and quickly sets her sights on Jeezra; her babysitter, lounging on the den sofa, engrossed in a sizable book simply titled "Enlightenment".

"Sorry I'm late Jeezra," Tara says, noticing the piece nestled in the 16 year old's lap.

"Oh its fine Mrs. T," the bi-racial teen responds.

Immersed in her read, Jeezra lost track of time and never noticed Tara's tardiness.

"You're a far better person than I am," Tara says, eyeing the book she judges to be at least seven hundred pages.

"It's really a good book, Mrs. T," the teen responds, knowing that to the average person, reading such a lengthy volume would be equivalent to watching grass grow.

"I will take your word for it," Tara says in a shrewd tone while retrieving a twenty-dollar bill from her wallet. The teen graciously takes the easy money.

"Tell your mom I said hi," Tara says as the teen gathers her things.

"I will," she responds. "I have been known to read tabloids from time to time," the teen says out of nowhere.

"Then I have to say stop hanging around Sara." Tara's rebuttal gets an instant outburst of laughter from the teen.

Afterwards, Tara heads up stairs. She enters a bedroom and finds her daughter Megan, lying face up on her bed. Her ears are connected to her iPod and her eyes are honed in on the cell phone screen as she texts at breakneck speed.

"Meg…Meg!"

Megan is interrupted from her intense texting session when she sees her mother standing in the doorway.

"Oh, hi Mom," she says disconnecting herself from her iPod.

The eleven year old is Tara's daughter with her husband Dale.

"Has your sister called today?"

"Hmm…let me see, she doesn't need money and she's not fighting with her so-called boyfriend. So no…she hasn't called today."

Tara eyes Megan sternly to show disapproval with her sarcastic tone.

"Did I tell you how wonderful it is to see you, Mother dear?" Megan asks with a gleaming smile. Finding humor in Megan's silly spectacle, Tara holds a poker face.

"Don't talk that way about your sister," she says, knowing there is much validity to her daughter's claim.

If you only knew the scary similarity in the early lives of Sara and Tara, her mind asserts.

"You've got another thirty minutes to stay up."

"Forty minutes, oh please! Please! Please!"

"Alright, alright, you've got forty minutes and then you hit the shower and get ready for bed."

"You know you're the world's best mom?"

"Why, absolutely child," Tara responds, with a big smile and a southern drawl.

She approaches the stairs and hears, "Mom! We need more Hot Pockets!

And milk! And cereal! Frosted Mini Crisps!"

As her daughter yells her wish list, Tara hears the clunk of the heavy oak front door. Walking downstairs, she gazes upon her husband Dale, who looks as if his day was no better than hers. The fifty year old is one of three partners of Sentinel Security, a small security firm they started after leaving law enforcement together, and while he and Tara were dating.

Of average height, he looks younger than his fifty years, but the stress of a competitive industry is starting to wear on the former two-time high school 145 lbs. State-wrestling champion. Barring the loss of her father and the Sexton case, Dale met Tara at the lowest point in her life. He introduced her to something she had never known until that point…sanity.

"I owe my life to the man I love," she often says in spite of the landmark achievements she has accomplished at Division.

For Dale, it was love at first sight and nothing has changed for him ever since. His previous marriage lasted five grueling years and produced no children, which he desperately wanted. After his divorce, he occasionally dated but vowed never to remarry, immersing himself completely into law enforcement. Meeting Tara changed all that, despite her being unlike anyone he typically dated, and having considerable baggage at the time. Tara became his one true love and the mother of the only thing more precious, their daughter Megan.

As much as Tara loves her husband, at times she sees glimpses of her parent's relationship. She promises herself her marriage will never end up like theirs. However, flashes of the possibility creep up from time to time and gnaw at her.

Dale perks up seeing his wife at the top of the stairs. "Sunshine still up?" he asks, arriving home a little later than normal.

"Yeah, she's in her room, but you better hurry."

Dale strolls upstairs meeting Tara halfway and walks into a kiss.

"Have you eaten yet?" she asks.

"Uh huh, I grabbed something on the way home."

"What?" Tara asks suspiciously.

"That's the scary part. I forgot. Something healthy no doubt, or I'd still remember."

"You're hopeless, you know that?" she says with a tender smile, shaking her head at Dale's trademark humor.

"I've been trying to tell you that for years," he says, continuing upstairs.

Later that night, Tara sees her husband is in the nether regions of consciousness as they lie under the plush comforter of their bed.

"You know, that's going to be a tough sell," he mumbles, after hearing Tara's serial killer theory. Dale's eyes are closed and he sinks deeper, on the verge of sleep. "It's going to be tough...way too early." Dale's voice fades into a light snore. Tara is wide-awake and looks at her sleeping husband. She lays back and focuses on the textured ceiling, which in time, becomes hazy.

A girl, less than school age, wakes in the middle of the night. Wearing a nightshirt, she walks out of her tiny room and into the dark hallway. She walks across the hall into a room where she sees her father sprawled unconscious on a bed, and an empty Seagram 7 bottle lying on the floor. She looks in the direction of the muffled sounds that brought her out of her sleep. The girl walks down the long hallway towards a dimly lit living room. She stands in plain sight at the entrance of the living room and stares at the sofa. Her mother lies nude on the floor. The sofa blocks the girl's vision from the waist down. Her mother's firm breasts bounce abruptly from repeated thrusts. Her head thrashes rhythmically on a thick bed of dark hair. She bites her lips to muffle her pleasure as she works her lover with authority. A handsome young man with thick black hair is on top of her with long muscular arms extended. Sweat glistens from the lean, faintly hairy body of the man at least ten years the mother's junior.

"Baby...I've never had any this good...Oh Yes!" he says passionately in a low voice. He looks toward the hallway and sees the dark haired girl with her eyes fixed on the spectacle. He looks down upon his lover. Seeing the stunning resemblance, and that the mother is oblivious to the girl's presence, he turns his sights again to the girl. Their eyes meet. The young man works the mother with even greater purpose, triggering an immediate response.

"Oh yes, that's it!" she moans.

He smiles at the girl before turning his full attention to her mother, working her madly, triggering an orgasm that exhausts him. He stares into his lover's face, and then makes eye contact again with the girl, who has stood motionless the entire time.

A grin fills his face and he gingerly puts a finger to his mouth exhaling a gentle, "Ssshhh, it's our little secret."

Tara emerges from her sleep as the ceiling comes into focus. Like nights before, her sheets are moist. Slowly, she feels her heart rate and breathing returning to normal. Blood, which just moments earlier was pooled between her legs, flows elsewhere and her nipples, previously erect, are receding. Dread hits her as she realizes what has happened. Worse, Tara is unable to stop it.

"I am not like you. I will never be like you," she whispers assertively.

She looks over at her husband, lying in a fetal position facing away from her, then looks at the flaming numbers of the digital clock on her night stand to see that it is three a.m. Tara turns to Dale and gives him a gentle rub on the shoulders. She rolls over and assumes her own fetal position.

The dark-haired girl is in early puberty. Her long lean frame, with a hint of womanhood, wears a white sleeveless nightshirt that falls just above her knees as she walks through the dark abyss. A heavy fog blankets the floor, shimmering as far as the eye can see. In the distance, she sees the radiant figure of a woman staring at her. Unafraid, the girl walks towards the woman as she sees the woman doing the same. Soon, the girl realizes the alluring figure, wearing a white silk slip, is her mother. The two finally meet, stopping less than a foot apart. They stare at one another as mother and daughter, yet strangers. The girl raises a hand to touch her mother and the woman mimics her movement. As their hands come together, the girl realizes that she is not touching her mother's hand but the smooth, cold surface of a reflective barrier. She moves her hands slowly in a circular motion and the woman's movements emulates her daughter's.

"Tara," the mother's voice echoes in a soft southern tone, prompting the girl to stop. She looks into her mother's dark piercing eyes with a face void of expression.

"Tara, child, is this a wall...or a mirror?"

CHAPTER 6

The "S" Word

Tara, Dale and Megan walk outside the front door of their home into a gorgeous clear morning. Tara and Dale kiss before they head off to work.

"I don't know how late I'll be tonight," Dale says, walking to his car. He stops and looks back at Tara standing with Megan. "Hey!" he calls out getting her attention. "I hope you're wrong about your theory...But if you're not..." They stare at each other, understanding the gravity of a serial killer in La Flore and the foreboding possibilities if her theory is true. Tara and Megan watch Dale drive off when she sees her neighbor Faye Woodard, who she has not seen in several weeks, walking to her car.

"Faye!" Tara exclaims, astonished, almost not recognizing her. Faye turns to her with a beaming smile and a well-deserved sense of accomplishment and rightfully so. The sleek size ten dresses she wears are far from the snug size eighteens that were the staple of her wardrobe several months earlier. The drastic reduction in clothing size is not the only change for the forty-seven year old real estate agent. Faye's doctor took her off her high blood pressure, cholesterol and diabetes medications. However, the change she considers the sweetest happened yesterday when a hot young bag boy graciously offered to bring her groceries to the car...tip free.

"Faye, you look fantastic!"

Megan interjects. "You really look great Mrs. Woodard."

"Now you're going to make me cry," Faye responds, fanning her face as tears well up in her eyes.

Tara approaches Faye, giving her a big hug.

"Thank you, Tara and thank you, Meg," Faye says trying to regain her composure.

"Well, my goal is to get into a size eight, but my clothes were getting so baggy I had to buy something in the meantime. I can't remember the last time I wore a size ten."

"Well, you're in them now and there is no time like the present!" Tara says with great admiration for Faye's stunning new look.

Later, Tara drops Megan off at a local youth center just a few blocks from their home, then skillfully maneuvers through the morning traffic, finally reaching the precinct. At her desk, she sifts through piles of documents, footnotes and photos with a different mindset. Instead of investigating two random homicides that lead nowhere, she is now looking for links connecting them. Detective Cummings interrupts.

"Hey, I heard what happened at Pathology yesterday with you and McVey."

Tara pauses for a moment. "Please…Not now," she says in a low tone while continuing to thumb through the heap of material in front of her.

"I'll get with you later. I think I know what's up with G.I. Joe," he comments in a devious tone. Tara looks up to find Cummins wearing a sly grin. Her look tells him that she is not amused. She continues her daunting task when a towering mass catches her peripheral vision. She looks up to see her boss, Commander Robert Johnson, walking towards his office.

"Commander," she shouts in an effort to get his attention. He immediately recognizes the voice among the office chatter and turns his sights to her desk.

"Ah, Detective Tanner…I need to see you in my office," he says in a voice as commanding as his six foot seven inch height.

She walks towards the commander's office and crosses paths with Detective McVey. They eye each other for a moment, then continue on their way. Tara enters the commander's office.

"Close the door and sit down," he says in a casual tone.

She closes the door and sits in a plush leather armchair.

"Speak, Kiddo."

The fifty-five year old hails from Detroit, Michigan and a standout basketball player at Michigan State. Though he had a keen talent for the sport, he possessed a deep passion for academics and had an ever-growing interest in criminal justice. The Portland Trailblazers had just selected him in the third round of the NBA draft when he got the tragic news. A State Patrol found his older brother Richard with a single gunshot wound to the head on a desolate interstate highway. An army sergeant, he was driving home on well-deserved leave to visit family and to congratulate his younger brother, of whom he was deeply proud. The heartbreaking loss of his brother, who was more like a second father, devastated him. Even more disheartening, no one ever found the killer. He served a three-year contract with the Trailblazers; fulfilling a childhood dream to play in the pros. Johnson chose not to continue his professional career after his contract ended. Turning down a lucrative offer, he chose to pursue law enforcement, in the city not far from the desolate highway where the patrolman found his brother.

"Commander, just hear me out. I know this sounds a bit premature, but I believe there is a connection between the Terri Gibson and Kelly Vogel murders," Tara says, sitting upright in the chair. The commander adjusts his chair, sliding closer to his sturdy oak desk to hear her more clearly. "Go on," he says; his body language clearly telling Tara she has his undivided attention.

"The wounds on the victims are different, but the MO of the wounds may indicate a similar mindset. I think Terri Gibson and Kelly Vogel met the same killer."

After a pause, "Are we talking the "S" word here?" asking for feedback to confirm what he just heard.

"Yes Commander, we are," Tara responds.

He places both hands on his forehead and runs them down his face, then reclines back in his chair. His large hands fall on his thighs as he sighs heavily.

"Detective, I was playing golf yesterday with Mayor Hondo and the Chief. They told the press we've practically solved both murders and the great city of La Flore need not worry about another random homicide. Now, you're telling me we may have a damn serial killer on our hands?"

There is silence. Tara watches the commander reflect on what he just heard. He exhales with another heavy sigh.

"How certain are you about this?" he asks, looking her straight in the eyes.

"Well, about sixty percent," she says warily, hating to be the bearer of bad news.

"This will not leave this office, understood?"

"Yes, Commander," she responds, nodding her head.

"Keep digging and give me something better than sixty percent. We don't need a serial killer in an upcoming election year, but we sure as hell don't need another fiasco."

The comment rattles Tara slightly as she feels he is referring to the Sexton Case.

"Sorry, Kiddo," he says. "That was not my intent."

"No need to apologize," Tara responds, knowing how often he has gone to bat for her over the years.

"Now that that's out of the way, what the hell's going on with you and McVey? I heard about the incident in Pathology. I won't have infighting among my detectives."

"Nothing Commander, we just had a misunderstanding that we're working out. It won't happen again," she says, not wanting to rat on McVey for instigating the confrontation.

"Make sure it doesn't, because you don't want me to get involved. Good day, Detective."

Tara walks out of the commander's office and immediately sees McVey sitting at his desk. She sees the look of concern on his face, wondering about what just transpired. He hears the voice of Detective Cummins standing behind him.

"Trust me, McVey," he says with coolness, "If Tanner had ratted on you, the commander would be ripping you a new one right now."

CHAPTER 7

Frank's Studio

It is midafternoon as Tara drives through light traffic towards Beaverton Business Park. She arrives and parks in front of a row of business condominiums. Tara exits her car, retrieves a gym bag from her trunk and heads towards a condominium with a sign that reads "Perrino's Elite Training." There are several reasons why La Florians use personal trainers. Looking at Tara, one would not see a physical need for her to have a trainer. She looks remarkably fit for a woman of forty, and someone who has never been involved in sports. In Tara's case, coping with stress and anxiety is part of her motivation. Frank Perrino's fast and furious training has helped her immeasurably since the loss of her father.

She walks into the state of the art studio that looks much larger than its modest appearance outside suggests. Entering, the beat of techno music from a satellite radio station greets her. She hears Frank already engaged in a training session.

"Hmm, sounds like he's in rare form today," she asserts, heading for the change room.

Minutes later, she walks briskly on a treadmill as his current session winds down. Tara's purple and black sports bra with matching leggings clearly displays a five foot seven, hundred and twenty eight-pound physique that after two years with Frank is lean, well-toned, deceptively strong and highly athletic.

A short stocky man in his mid-fifties emerges from the training floor with a Cheshire Cat-like grin on his face and drenched in sweat.

"I warmed him up for you!" he says enthusiastically.

"Apparently," Tara replies, curious as to whom she was speaking.

"My name is Chet, Chet Wellington." She immediately recognizes the Wellington name from Wellington, Carter and Associates, one of La Flore's big law firms.

"I'm Tara," returning the courtesy.

"Well Tara, as much as I'd like to stay and chat with someone as pretty as you, money calls."

"Can't argue with that," she says with a grin.

After Mr. Wellington leaves, a voice rings out, "Hey."

As Frank approaches, it becomes instantly evident why Tara has a trainer, or at least this particular trainer. Not only is Frank exceedingly handsome, but the resemblance he has to the young lover, the one she dreams of staring at her while having sex with her mother, is striking. Like Tara, Frank is not a native of La Flore. Sicilian born, his family moved to the US when he was seven. A scrawny four-eyed kid who was often picked on, Frank stumbled across his father's dusty set of free weights at the tender age of twelve. The rest is history. Now twenty-eight; his muscular six feet, two hundred pounds exudes profound power and sex appeal. With a chiseled, tanned face and a head of thick black hair, he could easily hold his own with the top male models.

From the look on her face, Frank knows immediately what she is thinking,

"Techno music?" Tara exclaims curious about Mr. Wellington's music selection.

Frank grins, shrugging his broad shoulders.

"Looks can be deceiving. You of all people should know that."

She gets off the treadmill and they walk into an embrace, much to each other's satisfaction.

"You're tense and stressed," Frank says with genuine concern, feeling her tension during their embrace.

"Yes, I am," she replies.

"Then you should have a great workout today," he proclaims.

Tara walks onto the training floor while Frank changes the satellite station to contemporary pop. The sound of Mariah Carey's hit "Make it Happen" more than adequately sets the tone for her, as it rings throughout the studio. Frank walks onto the floor with a well-used clipboard holding a master sheet with her training program, which after two years, is dialed to perfection. He looks and sees she is wearing her game face.

"Ok, Tara, total body, full counts. Are you up to it?"

"I'm definitely up to it," she replies with anticipation for her fix.

"Then let's do it!"

Wasting no time, she starts her ordeal by cranking out fifty hanging leg raises and immediately nails another fifty crunches on an abdominal machine loaded with forty pounds.

"Beautiful, let's tighten that tush," Frank says in a commanding voice.

He hands her a pair of forty-pound dumbbells and she cranks out a set of twenty alternating lunges. Her heart rate is now elevated as sweat beads on her skin. Tara glances at the wall clock to gauge her pace. Time passes as they go through a grueling series of leg and back exercises. Tara's body is now drenched in sweat as her stress levels drop and her endorphin levels rise.

"You're looking fantastic! Are you still with me?"

"I'm with you Frank," she says between heavy breaths, feeling the endorphin rush.

"Lie on the bench," he orders, now deep in his trainer's zone.

Tara lays face up on a flat bench while Frank retrieves an eighty pound barbell. He places the bar over her chest, nearly straddling her face.

"Here we go, Tara. Grab it," he commands.

Knowing what he wants, she grabs the barbell and assails a set of bench presses.

"Yes...that's good," Frank says with dark eyes locked on Tara's grimace.

Her breathing and grunting increase with each arduous repetition, while the muscles of her chest, shoulders and triceps burn to the edge of their tolerance.

"Oh Frank, I don't know," she calls out, hitting a wall on her eighth repetition.

"I know!" Frank asserts with authority. "Finish it Tara...I want ten!"

She blasts another rep and immediately concludes she has nothing left. Just as her arms began to give way to the unforgiving barbell,

"If you won't do it for yourself...do it for me."

The barbell descends once more and touches Tara's chest. In a final burst, she hurls the eighty-pound barbell upwards. Tara's muscles scream as the barbell creeps at a snail's pace.

"Get it...Get it...Get it Tara...Beautiful! That's my girl!"

Frank snatches the barbell from her hands. Exhausted but victorious, Tara's arms go limp and dangle from the bench.

"You ok? That was a hell of a finish," Frank comments, putting away the barbell.

"I…couldn't be better," she replies with closed eyes and a weary voice. "Remind me why I do this again."

"For starters, because you look fantastic. I've seen women in their twenties that would give up their first born to have your body. You're an intensity junkie and the training is your fix; that's where I come in. Finally, you never know what you may encounter that will require this level of training."

"Nothing in the foreseeable future," she says.

"How's your stress level now?" he asks with a smile.

"What stress level?" Tara responds, still lying on the bench.

After few minutes, Frank extends his hand. They clinch and Frank gently pulls Tara off the bench. Unexpectedly, she finds herself in his embrace. Tara feels the pronounced contours of his chest and abdominal muscles through the thin form-fitting shirt. Without thinking, she runs her fingers gingerly along his muscular back. Frank's breathing becomes heavy. His heart races, creating blood flow that becomes overtly apparent. From his expression, Tara senses he knows she is having the same reaction.

"Hey, we have to finish...training I mean," Tara says, barely able to get her words out.

"Yes...we do," Frank replies, battling struggles of his own.

Driving home, Tara's thoughts wrestle over her relationship with Frank. They have had minor flirtations before, but for her, this was too close for comfort. She feels frustration with a matter that is now very delicate. She admires and respects Frank's abilities as a trainer and all he has done for her, but knows the two are on a very slippery slope.

"How far do I let this go before I say enough?" Tara grudgingly asks herself. "Even more disturbing," she adds, "Do I want to?"

CHAPTER 8

The Assessment

Cassandra Lowden is a successful columnist for the La Flore Herald and several local magazines. A La Flore native, Cassandra was a five foot six, one hundred eighteen pound phenom and three-year captain of Woodland Hills High's powerhouse tennis team thirty years, three kids, and forty-nine pounds ago. Since her bitter divorce and a short lived Oxycontin addiction, Cassandra has been at odds with her torrid love affair with food, especially that of the starch and chocolate varieties. Puccini's, a four star La Flore restaurant, has a rich pasta Alfredo dish that Cassandra would gladly die for. Gifts Galore, a popular gift complex located at La Flore's Super Mall, stays well stocked with an assortment of decadent gourmet chocolates that Cassandra would gladly kill for.

A meticulous woman with an impeccable taste for fashion, Cassandra is an attractive woman in spite of her weight. This does not deter her from trying to, as she proclaims, "raise her stock," especially with the company of women she keeps. Over the years, Cassandra has tried countless diets, exercise programs and trainers. The long line of failures has formed a distorted yet resounding conclusion in her mind. An uncontrollable food addiction is not to blame for her woes with the scale. Instead, the diets, exercise programs, trainers and the four idiotic psychiatrists she hired, diagnosing her with an uncontrollable food addiction, are the culprits. Four months ago, an acquaintance she holds in high regard inspired

Cassandra to try yet another trainer. Her reasoning was simple; she could not possibly go wrong with a trainer who makes a sixty-one year old look as stunning as Thelma Carson.

Twelve weeks have passed and Cassandra has made little progress with the trainer Thelma raved about.

"I may not be giving him exactly a hundred percent but I am giving at least ninety five percent," she tells herself driving to the west side studio, with apprehension about her weekly assessment. "I haven't been to Gifts Galore in ten weeks…ten whole weeks! I should have dropped at least twenty pounds for that reason alone. Ok…I stocked up on a few boxes of chocolates but I have had no more than one or two per day. What can that possibly hurt?"

Cassandra does not read nutrition labels, especially when she is in need of a chocolate fix. She does not know that one of her delightful chocolates packs a whopping two hundred and fifty calories. One chocolate per day would have her consuming an extra seventeen hundred and fifty calories per week.

Cassandra finally arrives and parks her late model Lexus in front of the studio. Upon entering, she immediately sees her trainer. His composed demeanor masks emotions that after the twelve-week period, are now bordering rage.

"I know, I know…I'm ten minutes late. I'll hurry," she says, scurrying past the trainer to the change room.

"You're my last client for the day Cassandra; please take your time," he says calmly.

He observes her, scurrying to meet her appointment, and sees someone who has him at the end of his rope. Had she turned for a moment to see his dark and threatening stare, Cassandra Lowden would surely have thought twice about attending her assessment.

Minutes later, she stands in front of the doctor's scale as if about to walk to the gallows.

"Ok, Cassandra, let's step up."

She stands cautiously on the scale that confirms the tip he had received from his receptionist. Becky had seen Cassandra just three nights earlier at El Fiesta's with a small group of girlfriends. She recalls one of the women, privy to her training, calling her out on the copious Fiesta Special she had just ordered.

"Oh...It's my cheat meal. I get one cheat meal a week," *she says, addressing the group.*

"That cheat meal includes two grand margaritas?" a *woman from the group interjects. Eyes roll accompanied by* *subtle grins. One woman excuses herself to vent her* *amusement.*

Cassandra shakes her head in disbelieve as the scale has her three pounds heavier than her last assessment.

"I've had it. I've followed your program for twelve weeks and it didn't work," Cassandra says out of frustration. "I don't know why I fall for these ridiculous programs!" Tears well in her eyes.

"Cassandra," the trainer says in a calm, deliberate tone. "I need to ask you something and you need to be truthful, did you follow the changes we made three weeks ago?"

"Yes…I did," she says.

"Cassandra," the trainer says in a deliberate, not so calm tone, "did you do something…three days ago…You know…have a cheat meal with margaritas, perhaps?"

Cassandra goes on the offensive.

"I don't like your tone and I don't like what you're insinuating. I followed your program and it didn't wor…"

Cassandra's last word did not materialize before she finds herself four feet from where she was standing, jammed against a wall, with a powerful hand clamped over her mouth.

When her mind catches up to what has happened, she finds herself gazing into eyes that are cold and dark. Astonishment instantly becomes fear, then terror when she realizes she is in a deadly place. The eyes peering at her are not the eyes of the man she was with moments ago.

"That was not the answer to my question Cassandra; a simple yes or no would have sufficed!"

Tears began to stream heavily down Cassandra's face and the powerful hand muffles any chance of her screaming.

"I think you were insinuating my program didn't work, which means you were following your diet."

Adrenaline surges through Cassandra and her heart is beating at a frantic pace.

"Since you refuse to answer my question, I'm going to have to find out for myself. Now, you're probably wondering…How am I going to do that?"

Cassandra's inability to look down, spares her briefly as the skillful incision starts just above her groin, making quick work of her light clothing. The incision moves effortlessly upward, ending below her breastbone. He holds the razor sharp scalpel stained in blood within Cassandra's sight. She immediately panics as the long incision widens, exposing globules of fat below her skin. Cassandra begins to go into shock, her eyes become glazed and her body convulses.

"Not so fast," he says abruptly. "I need you to see my point."

Repeated incisions methodically cut through layers of fat. A final incision slices through thin abdominal muscles exposing Cassandra's delicate organs. The smell of innards is pungent and fills the room. The trainer, covered in blood, lays Cassandra's limp body on the floor. Gazing down at the gruesome sight, the trainer is distraught that he was unable to convey his point.

"Wake up, Cassandra," he says in a commanding tone. "I need you to wake up." He kneels down looking into unresponsive eyes. "Wake up!" He yells grabbing and violently shaking the lifeless body.

Disappointed at getting no response, he shoves Cassandra's body onto the floor where it emits a loud thud. He looks down upon his grisly work, without feeling a hint of remorse. He stares at the motionless face and dead eyes, only to view them as…pathetic.

"That's just like you, Cassandra," he says with contempt, "Always quitting when the going gets tough."

CHAPTER 9

Are You About to Kill Again?

'*We provide local news like no one else...period! This is KAPO 7 News with Anchorwoman Ashley Craig.*"

"*Good evening. We have the latest on the tragic breaking story earlier today. The gruesome discovery of yet another body within a three-month period has some La Florians asking the unthinkable. Is there a serial killer loose in La Flore? Carol Chase is on the scene.*"

"*Barbara Jones was walking home from a bridge game at a friend's house. She never made it,*" the newswoman reports. "*Last night between this location and her home, less than a block away, someone abducted her, took her to the woods you see behind me, and...well, the rest is too graphic to describe. Local children playing in those woods discovered her early this afternoon. Residents here are shocked, scared and outraged.*"

"*Barb was the most caring person I'd ever known,*" a resident and close friend proclaims, trying to muster strength to eulogize the victim. "*She was always the first person volunteering to lead the neighborhood toy drive and...*" The middle-aged woman fans her face in a vain attempt to control her emotions. Placing her hand on the camera lens, "*I can't do this...I'm sorry.*"

Another resident is more assertive.

"*The son of a bitch who did this to Barb just got a first class, one way express ticket to hell!*"

"There seems to be some consensus among residents that the murder of Barbara Jones may be linked to the Terry Gibson and Kelly Vogel killings."

"I wouldn't be surprised if there were a link," one resident states.

"Whether La Flore has a serial killer or not, one thing is certain, this quiet neighborhood must say their goodbyes to a beloved resident, heal and move on. Back to you, Ashley."

"This latest event may land Mayor Saks and Chief Nirez in hot water after a casual interview a few weeks earlier," the anchor says in a foreboding tone. "Both insisted La Florians should not worry about another random homicide. They are scheduled to hold a press conference about that interview, tomorrow."

***

An overcast morning sky, along with light drizzle, adds a dreary tone to La Flore's landscape. Tara weaves through the morning traffic with images of yesterday's crime scene and the killer's gruesome handiwork on Barbara Jones, fixed in her head. They discovered her lying face up with her stomach opened by an incision from her groin to her chest. Her abdominal cavity was emptied and her internal organs were scattered about. According to Agent Sumner, she could have lived through much of her ordeal. Tara reasons that it pales in comparison to the emotional trauma the small group of eight to ten year olds suffered, upon seeing their grisly find. Barbara Jones is dead, but the kids who found her have to live with the shocking images left by a harbinger of death, for the rest of their lives.

So much for sixty percent, Tara's mind concludes. *As far as she is concerned, the killer's horrid signature said it all.* Her phone rings, taking her attention. Tara sees it is Commander Johnson.

"Yes, Commander."

"How far are you from the precinct?"

"About ten minutes."

"When you get here, come straight to my office, understood?"

Tara has never received a call from the commander while on a morning commute to the precinct. In this case, she is not surprised. After watching the news commentary last night, Dale made a sarcastic remark about his need to stay at least ten feet from her to avoid the stench since shit was about to hit the fan at Division.

I'm sure he was paid a visit by the Chief, maybe even the Mayor, she tells herself with the precinct now in full view.

When Tara arrives, the scene at Division is more subdued than she had expected. The only indication of a crisis of any sort was the imposing figure of Chief Nirez, sitting in Commander Johnson's office. It is common to see La Flore's "Top Cop" drop by Division, but in light of last night's news, the detectives know this is not a casual visit. Tara has a captive audience when she walks towards the commander's office. As she approaches, she is relieved to hear laughter between them.

Commander Johnson sees her approaching and gestures her into his office.

"Close the door, Detective," he says casually.

The chief is sitting in a chair with his back to her. He springs from his chair, turns to face her and extends a hand of greeting. His immaculate, well-tailored, highly decorated uniform more than complements his average frame and less than average height, making him appear larger than life. What is most striking about La Flore's "Top Cop" is the full head of thick jet-black hair for a man of sixty.

"Detective Tanner, good to see you again," the chief says, engulfing Tara's hand in a vigorous handshake.

"How's Dale?" he asks enthusiastically.

"Dale is doing fine, Chief," Tara responds respectfully.

"You tell him his badge is always waiting for him if he decides to come back."

"I'm sure he knows it, Chief,"

As they sit and settle in their chairs, Tara perceives a shift to a more serious mood.

"I take it you saw the news last night," the commander says.

"Yes, I did."

Tara hesitates for a moment, "I'm one hundred percent certain that Terri Gibson, Kelly Vogel and Barbara Jones faced the same killer," she says with confidence.

Commander Johnson and Chief Nirez stare at each other and are visibly uneasy hearing Tara's remark.

"The wounds on each of the victims are the killer's signature. These are vendetta wounds and they're very personal, like the killer knows each victim intimately; but there's no one I can find to connect them."

"Or...they may be proxies for the killer's intended victims," a voice replies as if putting in the final piece of a puzzle.

The chief's comment catches both Tara and the commander off guard.

"Do you have anything else to report, Detective?" the commander asks.

"No, that's all I have at the moment," Tara replies, still curious about the chief's comment.

"You may leave Detective, and close the door behind you, please."

As Tara closes the door, an awkward silence fills the office between the chief and commander.

"Is there anything you'd like to share with me Chief?" the commander asks, his curiosity peaked.

"I don't know. Somehow, her words reminded me of a case a fellow detective and very close friend of mine had when I was a junior detective. He said those words almost verbatim. I could be wrong but, it's just a feeling I have. I can't explain it."

"You mean, the case where the detective and very close friend was killed by the suspect he was pursuing?"

"Yeah, that case," the chief says.

"You know, she might be on to something with these murders," Johnson asserts.

"She might. We both thought that during the Sexton case," the chief rebuts.

"That was then," Johnson quickly counters.

"Well, let's hope our good detective has finally got her mojo back," the chief says.

Silence fills the room again as the game of devil's advocate reaches an impasse. Chief Nirez gives a deep sigh.

"The statements Hondo and I made about the two killings weren't supposed to leave that golf course. Leave it to those Liberal fucks and their drive-by media to try to screw us in an election year. I will inform Hondo of the situation. Keep me informed."

"Will do."

"How will you handle the press conference this afternoon?" Johnson asks.

"As best we can. Speaking of which, duty calls," the chief exclaims as the two men rise from their chairs.

The chief walks purposefully towards the office door.

"Bob," he says stopping at the door.

"Yes, Chief."

"We have to move quickly on this, but we absolutely cannot fuck this up...*Comprendi?*"

"I know, Chief."

Later, Tara is at her desk when the chief exits the commander's office and walks by placing a hand on her shoulder.

"Give my regards to Dale," he tells her in a low voice.

"I will, Chief," Tara says watching him exit.

"Hey, what happened in there?" Cummins asks from his desk adjacent to Tara.

"I told them I'm a hundred percent certain that the three victims met the same killer."

"That's it?" Cummins asks.

Tara gives a sigh. "The chief made an off the wall comment, but other than that," she shrugs her shoulders.

"Man…gossip isn't what it used to be around here," Cummins says.

He turns to face the mound of paperwork on his desk.

Tara stares at Cummins for a moment. She reflects on the statement the chief made in the commander's office, not knowing why. She pulls up to her desk grabbing a folder containing the crime scene photos of Gibson, Vogel and Jones. As Tara thumbs through the photos, she replays the countless interviews she conducted over the past weeks in her mind. She remembers the devastation inflicted on the families and friends of the victims.

I need something. I need anything, she tells herself. *What is your name Mr. Killer? I say Mr. because you are a man; that I'm sure of.*

Tara closes the folder and tosses it on her desk. Her mind continues to ponder.

Would I know you, if I saw you? Have I seen you already? Do you know the degree of suffering and misery you are causing? Are you about to kill again?

CHAPTER 10

Thank You for the Head

"Is there anything you need from me before I go?" Becky asks.

"No. Enjoy the rest of your day," the trainer responds mechanically, lost in thought.

"Are you ok?" Becky asks.

"Yes, yes I'm fine."

"Don't forget, Wanda rescheduled her appointment for Thursday instead of tomorrow morning."

"Oh yeah, that's right, I almost forgot. Thanks for reminding me, Becky. Thanks for a lot of things. That is why I order you to enjoy the rest of your day."

"Yes, sir," Becky snaps. Her response brings a grin and chuckle from her boss as she heads out the door.

He looks at the wall clock seeing that it is ten minutes before the hour and the arrival of his next client. He also sees it is time to end a deep festering resentment that has finally reached its breaking point. His mind flashes back three months earlier.

***

He is in the middle of an intense morning session with a long time client. The client smells of alcohol from a party the previous night, but amazingly, is able to perform the grueling session.

"Are you still with me?" he asks, smelling alcohol on the client's breath and through streams of sweat.

"I feel great. I always feel great when I'm with you," the client responds affectionately.

The trainer is uncomfortable. This is not the same client he has trained for nearly two years. He realizes the client is still under the influence despite his ability to train at a high level. As the session concludes, the client is exhausted.

"That was great. You're the best trainer I've ever had. Thank you, thank you so much." The client catches him off guard with an embrace that quickly becomes more than friendly. He pushes the client away.

"I'm sorry, I didn't mean that. Please forgive me. It won't happen again, I promise," the client says in desperation.

Two nights ago, he received a phone message. It was the voice of the client, clearly intoxicated.

"I just want you in my bed, to give you head. You're so sexy." Drunken laughter follows. There is silence, then sadness.

"What the hell am I doing? You don't want me. I'm not your type."

***

The slam of the door brings the trainer back to the present as his client rushes in, heading towards the change room.

"I'll be quick," says Jacob Nelson, owner of a small construction company, husband and father of three.

Walking onto the training floor, eager to train and very sober, Jacob asks, "What's the order for the day, boss?"

"We'll do back and biceps. Sound like a plan?"

"Sounds like a good plan, along with some AC/DC," Jacob responds.

He does not recall his past displays of affection towards the trainer because alcohol gives him blackouts. He also does not realize what he has set in motion, and that the other man in the room has desires of his own.

"We'll do integrated training and start with lats," the trainer says in a business like tone.

"Thunder Struck" fills the studio as the trainer sends Jacob through a series of warm up sets before shifting the training into overdrive. Eight minutes into the intense session, Jacob peels off the light sweatshirt displaying a streamline physique, lean arms and muscular shoulders through his soaked tank top. The trainer takes Jacob through an unforgiving gauntlet of sets in rapid succession engorging his muscles with blood, his heart pounding in his chest.

"Are you with me, Jake?" he asks in an assertive tone.

Waging war on the training floor is nothing new to Jacob. It is the main reason he is a client at Fit Now

Personal Training. For the first time, this intensity junkie is training beyond his tolerance.

"I'm…I'm with you, Boss," Jacob says between gasps and with slight hesitation.

"I know you haven't been here before, but you can handle it. I know you can," he asserts sensing Jacob's apprehension.

With his trainer's words of encouragement, and never being one to back down from a fight, Jacob assails another five sets with brutal intensity before collapsing on the floor.

He lies face up with arms and legs outstretched as if making a snow angel.

"That was very good Jake. I knew you could do it; but we're not finished. Look at the clock."

Jacob eyes the clock and is stunned to see there is still ten minutes left of his session. "What else do we have?" Jacob asks out of curiosity.

"A few more sets, then lower back. It'll be over with before you know it."

Jacob quickly drains his half-full water bottle, his heart rate and breathing coming back to normal. The surge of endorphins finally catches up to Jacob's torrid training pace and he feels its euphoric effects. getting a second wind, Jacob is ready.

"Ok…Let's do it."

He battles through three heavy sets of dumbbell rows with surprising ease and is clearly in another training zone.

"You're looking outstanding, Jake. Let's finish with lower back." Jacob heads to a black ominous looking apparatus and the trainer retrieves a fifty-pound dumbbell.

Jacob steps onto the apparatus that has him standing at a forty-five degree angle. Pads pressed against his heels and thighs stabilize him and keep him from falling. Jacob can feel his lower back engage just in holding himself up. The trainer holds the dumbbell to Jacob's chest. Jacob cradles the dumbbell with strong hands.

"Are you ready, Jake?" he asks. Jacob gives a firm nod and focuses on the upcoming task. "Attack!" The trainer barks, sending Jacob to his last grueling set.

After the punishing session, "Open your eyes, Jake."

Jacob opens his eyes while lying face up on the floor and sees the trainer standing over his head holding the fifty-pound dumbbell. Jacob looks at him and smiles.

"That was a great workout, Boss," he says, endorphins coursing through him.

The trainer responds with a grin before returning the dumbbell. Jacob slowly stands up and walks towards the change room.

"You know, Boss, this was the best workout I've ever…"

As Jacob turns to face the trainer, the speed, force, density, sharpness and perfect swing of the heavy cleaver was too much for the skin, muscle, cartilage and bone that it severed effortlessly. With one vicious swing, Jacob's head becomes a tumbling mass, separated from its body.

The headless frame remains standing as blood spews violently from the wound, spraying the ceiling. Jacob's hands instinctively grasp the severed neck in disbelief. The headless body convulses and an arm extends, reaching out to the trainer. It takes one lumbering step forward, before collapsing to the floor, lying motionless. The trainer sees that the head has rolled a few feet and settled next to the leg press, leaving a trail of blood and gore. He walks over to the leg press and retrieves the head, holding it in both hands. He stares at the blank face and sad eyes, now partially closed. In a heavy, sinister voice he utters,

"Thank you, Jake. Thank you so much for the head."

CHAPTER 11

La Florians Live in Fear

The gruesome discovery of Cedric Wells, a senior at La Flore City University, sends a shockwave of emotions throughout the city. The family of the victim and La Flore's gay community perceive his decapitation as a heinous hate crime, since Cedric was openly and proudly gay. Some see their portentous suspicion now a grim reality: their beloved city is in the grips of a reaper of death, a serial killer. Others see La Flore as a pristine city that has had it better than good for so long; it is merely it's time to experience a crisis of this scope. Many feel outraged and betrayed by the hubris displayed by Mayor Hondo and Chief Nirez. The statements they made on the golf course are now coming back to haunt them. For most La Florians, one thing is certain, whether it is a serial killer or a surge of random homicides, LFPD appears to have made no headway since the discovery of the body of Terri Gibson. For the first time in a generation, La Florians live in fear.

Fear and despair for some, are opportunities for others. In a fiery town hall speech, Democratic Mayoral candidate Eddie Lamar seizes that opportunity to attack the Mayor and Chief.

"Mayor Saks and Chief Nirez, while lounging and playing golf, told us the murders of our fellow citizens were solved and that we did not have to worry about anymore random homicides. Well, since then, we have lost two more La Florians in a most vile and vicious way. Now, we know the truth is that they are no closer to solving anything since

finding the body of Terri Gibson in Sheridan Park. Terri was a friend, a mentor and a credit to our great city. They have lied to us, and they have failed us. It is time for them to go. It is time for new leadership."

Mayor Hondo and the chief's less than stellar performance at their press conference, Eddie Lamar's relentless attacks and their double-digit drop in the polls paint a grim picture for the duo as the election looms.

At Division, frustration mounts as the lack of evidence and witnesses leave them clueless as to what actions to take.

"I need you to work your magic, Kiddo, and soon," Commander Johnson tells Tara.

She knows as well as the rest of the detectives that despite his calm demeanor, the commander is under enormous stress. Tara is quite familiar with this type of stress as she watched it destroy her father. She also knows the cat and mouse game played between hunter and serial killer, though she has never faced one until now.

"This murderer has claimed four victims. That's two victims away from the notorious Son of Sam killer," Tara says, tallying the score aloud in a low voice.

"Charles Hatcher claimed sixteen victims, Jeffery Dahmer, seventeen victims and that sick bastard Andrei Chikatilo claimed fifty-three victims."

Instantly recognizing the voice, she pauses for a moment before turning to face her surprise guest.

"Chikatilo is out," she asserts.

"If our friend claims the lives of fifty-three La Florians I will personally take a knife and slit my own throat. And you?"

"Well, being the outdoorsy type, I guess I will jump off a cliff, no chute of course."

"Our killer will not reach the status of Hatcher or Dahmer."

"Sounds like a good plan," her guest concurs.

He turns and walks away.

After a few feet, Tara calls to him, "Detective McVey!"

He stops, turns and faces her.

"Thanks for the history lesson, Detective."

He flashes a grin, and then walks away.

She looks over at her desk at Detective Cummins. He smiles, nodding his head in approval. She walks towards her desk wearing a pleasant face. Cummins takes his right hand and simulates a pistol shot. He falls back in his chair, both hands dangling by his side. Tara rolls her eyes. She walks the short distance to her desk while Cummins remains sprawled in his chair. As she approaches, he sits up.

"That's how I'd do it, not that crazy crap you and McVey were talking about."

Detective Cummins grabs his Glock.

"Just put the little darling in your mouth, a little squeeze on the trigger and presto; pure and simple."

Tara retrieves her keys from her desk, looks at Cummins and shakes her head.

"What?" he responds, throwing his hands up as he watches her disappear from sight.

It is three a.m. and Tara is in the middle of a deep sleep. Her dream is a rollercoaster, a myriad of scenes, sounds and voices that reverberate incoherently, at times making her flinch.

Bells toll ominously as Tara stands along the road of a cemetery. The scene is overcast, gloomy and surreal. She watches the funeral procession of the victims pass her by, only to see the weathered tombstones of Sally and "Little Tim" Sexton in front of her.

"Ashes to ashes, dust to dust," a grim voice echoes. The sound of dirt falling on a closed casket resonates with striking detail.

"Whoever did this is one evil son of a bitch."

She sees an ominous shadow of a man but cannot make him out.

"I need something...I need anything...That wound is more than just a wound...It's a signature...We sure as hell don't need another Sexton fiasco."

Tara finds herself at her desk while grisly photos of the victims fall like autumn leaves around her.

Who would do this to my baby?...She got her brains bashed out...I need you to work your magic, Kiddo and soon...These may be proxies for the true victims.

She sees a nine year old girl walking aimlessly towards her looking as if she has seen a ghost. "The boogey man got Mrs. Jones. He opened her up," the girl says. "He's over there." Tara's sight follows the girl's pale withered finger pointing to a wood line. Again, she sees the spectral figure staring at her holding a blood-soaked knife. She steps in front of the girl, shielding her as she engages in a face-off.

The dark figure raises a hand plainly displaying four fingers.

That's two victims away from the notorious Son of Sam Killer, she hears a voice echo. Tara becomes enraged. "Chikatilo is out!" she yells. "You will never reach the status of Hatcher or Dahmer, you fucking coward! I will nail your ass and enjoy watching you fry while sipping a cold one!"

The specter remains motionless. Then, heavy, sinister laughter rings deafeningly throughout. Tara quickly draws her Glock and releases a hail of bullets in its direction. As the din of gunfire dissipates, the figure remains unmoving. It looks away, pointing the blood-soaked knife in the same direction.

Tara's gaze follows the knife to the barrier where she last saw her mother. Instantly, she is transported mere inches away from it, clearly seeing her reflection on its surface. She runs her hands across the smooth plane, and then sees an image come into focus. It is her parent's living room sofa. Her mother is nude, straddling the sofa with her arms outstretched across its back and her knees spread on its pillows. She stares intensely at her daughter, as if she were finally privy to an enticing secret.

"Now, Tara, you naughty thang," she says in a seductive southern tone.

"When were you going to tell me about your friend...hmm?"

Tara steps back and sees Frank's nude muscular body and full erection emerge from the shadows and approaching her mother from behind. Tara's heart races as Frank's eager member accommodates her mother.

"I believe you've picked a winner, child. He looks so much like my young stud Phil. It's amazing, he kinda feels like him too."

She looks on as Frank pounds her mother ferociously.

"Tara, I hate to be rude, but I'm going to be distracted for a moment. Girl stuff, you know how it is."

Tara watches her mother release an intense orgasm. Afterwards, the mother observes Tara's expression as she gazes upon the carnal spectacle.

"Wait, wait a minute. You two haven't done it yet," the mother says, slightly astonished. "Oh Tara, oh yes, I'm about to cum," Frank says, barely able to contain himself. His words draw Tara's attention.

"Why, he thinks I'm you. I'm so jealous," her mother says in a patronizing tone.

"Two years and you haven't tried this young stud? You do not know what you are missing, and believe me, I think he really likes you."

The two are startled as Frank releases an intense eruption before collapsing helplessly, disappearing back into the shadows.

"See, I told you."

A puzzled look takes hold of her mother's face.

"You know, as much as I enjoyed your...trainer," she says gesturing quotes with both hands, "There's something about this I can't quite put my finger on."

Tara looks away, mortified and heartbroken at what she has just witnessed.

"Tara, Tara child," her mother calls out, trying to get her attention. Her daughter glances at her with disgust.

"The gentleman behind you would like to have a word with you."

Tara sees the reflection of the specter in the barrier now standing directly behind her. Shocked, she sees the knife that was in his hand, is now in hers. Faster than she can think and unable to control her hands, Tara reaches behind her head, hearing bone crunch and tendons snap as her shoulder separates. She grabs her hair, cruelly jerking her head back, exposing a delicate neck. Tara is completely helpless as the sharp blade guides her hand and makes quick work as she slits her own throat. The blade slices cleanly through flesh and cartilage. Blood pools rapidly as a horrid gurgle emanates from the gash.

Tara gasps, springing from her sleep. She pants as her heart hammers in her chest. She frantically feels around her neck and shoulders for blood and deformities.

"Tara, are you alright?" Dale yells hearing the commotion over a raging shower.

After a moment, "I'm fine."

Tara sits up, her heart finally settles and her breathing is calm. Scanning the familiar surroundings of her bedroom, she realizes the bizarre and vivid events she just experienced were mere fantasy...a nightmare. Her frustration of being outwitted by an elusive killer, the fear of being like her mother, her feelings about Frank and her controversial past collide, leaving her listless and demoralized. She grabs a pillow and collapses onto her bed covering her head to block out an oppressive world. Lying in the fetal position, she feels unwilling to face another day.

CHAPTER 12

The Light Comes On

Weeks pass before the killer strikes again. To Tara, the morning crime scene looks surreal, like a Clive Barker movie on steroids.

"If this is your killer, Agent Tanner, then he left one hell of a signature," Agent Sumner says assessing the carnage.

His CSI team meticulously processes the area. The victim, Penny Keester, is a writer of children's books. Her friend and co-author Kathy Maddox found her in her Woodland Hills home. Now, Kathy lies somewhere between shock and madness after seeing Penny's bedroom walls smeared in blood and pieces of flesh and her body bludgeoned beyond recognition.

"If I didn't know any better I'd think someone threw a grenade in here," McVey comments. The bloodbath brings back graphic memories of his tours in Baghdad.

"You know, this doesn't strike me as the work of the same killer," Detective Cummins adds.

"The other killings were heinous but clean; even the woman who was gutted. What was her name again?"

"Barbara Jones," McVey replies.

After a few moments, "Hey Tanner, you haven't said two words since you've been here," Cummins says.

"It's that time again," Tara replies in a somber tone.

"What time? That time of the month?" Cummins asks.

They stare at each other for a moment. It does not take long for Cummins to see the significance of the day written on Tara's face.

"Oh, that time." Cummins responds, finally realizing the day marked the third anniversary of the loss of her father. To his chagrin, "I'm sorry, Tanner."

"It's ok, Cummins, really. You're right about one thing; our killer isn't usually this sloppy." Tara looks around to survey the crime scene again before fixing her sights upon the grisly work on the bedroom floor. "Call me crazy, Cummins, but I still think this is our guy," Tara says after a moment of silent deliberation.

Later that afternoon, Tara drives through heavy traffic. The anxiety over her father and the frustration of being one upped by an evasive killer converge on her emotions and her psyche. Overwhelmed, she pulls over for a moment to regain her composure. With her forehead on the steering wheel, her eyes began to well up with tears.

"How can this person kill with impunity? I'm better than this!"

She holds back the urge to go into a full throttle cry and collects herself.

"I could sure use some words of wisdom and encouragement now, Daddy. I really miss you."

Arriving home, Tara walks into Megan's room, finding her engaged in a heated text session.

"Meg, can you spend just a little time away from that damn phone!"

"Mom, I'm just…"

"Don't!" Tara snaps. "Did you empty the dishwasher like I told you?"

Megan looks stunned. "No, Mom, I'm sor…"

"Right, Meg!" Tara snaps again. She storms to the kitchen. The clanging of dishes and utensils ring out as she performs the task she had given to Megan. Finishing, she feels a strong presence in the room. She turns suddenly.

Startled, Tara sees Megan standing in the kitchen. Her face is flushed and her dark piercing eyes are intense and fixed on her mother. Tara has never seen this expression on her daughter, making her appear much older than her eleven years.

After a moment, an assertive voice proclaims, "I miss him too, Mom." Tears began to well in Megan's eyes. Tara clearly sees her daughter's anguish, that in a fit of anger, she failed to see earlier. Tara falls to her knees. In a rush, the full throttle cry she managed to avoid earlier engulfs her. Mother and daughter soon embrace and succumb to heartfelt sobs.

"I'm sorry, Meg, I love you so much."

"It's ok, Mom. I love you too."

Later, Tara's oldest daughter, Sara, joins them. Sara's emotions over her grandfather fuel another outburst amongst mother and daughters.

It is late evening when Dale arrives. He walks into the den and the sight before him is indisputable. Popcorn, chocolate, a stack of chick flicks and three women in socks, huddled on the sofa.

"Damn, I've landed on Venus," he says aloud. "Well, how goes it ladies?" he asks in a feeble attempt to mask clearly being the odd man out.

"Hi Dad. Hi Dale. Hi honey," is said in perfect unison as their eyes remain locked on the flat screen. The movie "Ghost" is starting to heat up. Seeing his presence has no impact...whatsoever. He heads for the stairs, "I'm going to my cave and later, I'll ward off predators."

Megan gives her father a baffled look. He comments under his breath as he walks up stairs. "Now, would be a good time for a son."

Hours later, Sara curls in a ball asleep on one end of the sofa. Megan is still up with her mother, although it is way past her bedtime.

"Turn off the DVD while I get some blankets for your sister."

When Tara returns, she finds Megan watching the late news on the most recent murder victim. The photo of Penny Keester on the large screen draws her attention as family and friends eulogize the victim. Megan hits the power switch prompting the large screen to instantly go black.

"That's so sad," she tells her mother.

"It's very sad," Tara responds.

"You know, Mom, after seeing her picture, if I didn't know any better; I'd swear she was Mrs. Woodard."

Megan gives her mother a hug before heading upstairs to bed, unaware of what she had just said. In an instant and for reasons unknown, time freezes for Tara, the light comes on.

Minutes later, Faye Woodard is in a plush house robe as she strolls to answer her door, curious to who could be visiting her at this time of night. Upon opening the door, "Tara, is everything ok?" she asks, a bit concerned about her surprise visit. "Please come in," she says gesturing her inside.

"I'm so sorry for the inconvenience, Faye, and I promise this won't take long," Tara says standing just inside the doorway.

"My, you're looking great, Faye," Tara exclaims.

"Oh, I fell off the wagon a bit so I'm up about five pounds. I do not think Daniel took it too well. He can be pretty anal at times, but I guess that's why he's such a great trainer."

"Actually, that's why I'm here. I have a girlfriend that is looking for a good trainer and since Daniel, you did say Daniel, right?"

"Yes, his name is Daniel, Daniel Wade," Faye responds.

"Since Daniel Wade has done such a fantastic job with you, and Frank…"

"Who's Frank?" Faye interjects.

"Oh, Frank is my trainer."

"You have a trainer? Oh, get out!" she says and the two share a fit of laughter.

"I thought you knew!"

"If I had known you had a trainer, Tara, I would have gotten one a long time ago!"

"Well, Frank…my trainer is not taking on any more clients so I was wondering if Daniel… your trainer, would be able to help."

"Let me get you his business card. I've got a bunch here somewhere."

Faye walks off in earnest. Moments later, she returns with a glossy business card and hands it to Tara.

"Here you go. Should I let him know your friend is coming?" Faye asks.

"Oh, that won't be necessary. He'll know when they meet. Thank you so much, Faye, and hope I wasn't an inconvenience."

"Not at all, Tara, and hope I was helpful."

Tara holds up the business card between two fingers.

"We shall see."

They exchange goodnights. Tara walks the short distance to her front door and stops. *Hmm, Daniel Wade*, she says to herself. Tara holds the white business card under the door light, examining the red lettering that reads, "Fit Now Private Personal Training."

CHAPTER 13

Harry

The next morning, slogging in the hallway from the bathroom, Megan, groggy and hung-over from last night's experience, is suddenly ambushed by a bear hug.

"Thank you, Meg!"

"Sure thing, Mom," she responds instinctively, half-asleep.

Incoherent and oblivious to Tara's gratitude, Megan staggers back to the warmth and comfort of her bed. Tara walks downstairs where her older daughter has cleaned the den and grabbed a quick bite.

"I didn't want to disturb anybody," Sara says, gathering her things.

"No, no, we're fine," her mother asserts.

With a startling resemblance, the two look like older and younger sisters rather than mother and daughter.

Knowing talk of relationships is a slippery slope, Tara says, "So, journalism, huh?"

"Yep, I figure if my mom can be a great detective, why can't I be a great journalist?"

Tara has a strong desire to ask Sara whether she was planning on pursuing tabloid journalism. However, after last night's bonding, she is in no mood to deal with the argument that could result.

"I've got to go, Mom," Sara says, glad her mother did not pursue the subject, though sure it probably crossed her mind. After last night, she too, is in no mood for drama.

The two embrace and Tara hopes her daughter's life has reached a turning point. Sara kisses her mother on the cheek. "Tell Meg and Dale bye for me."

"I will," Tara says lovingly.

Her daughter walks to the door.

"You know, I've worked with quite a few journalists. Who knows, maybe one day we may work a case together," Tara says.

Arriving at the door, Sara stops, turns, and faces her mother.

"Tara and Sara Tanner, working a case together; now that's a scary thought," she says with a slight grin.

Later that morning, Tara arrives at the precinct and heads straight to the Intelligence Division. There, she sees a longtime acquaintance, Agent Stephanie Jenkins, head of the division.

"Detective Tanner, long time since I've seen your face," Agent Jenkins says, finishing a team meeting. "To what do I owe this pleasure?"

"I need a background check on a Daniel Wade."

Tara hands Agent Jenkins the business card she received from Faye Woodard and the agent makes a quick scan of the name spelling.

"What's the purpose of the inquiry on Mr. Wade?"

"Murder suspect," Tara responds.

"You mean, you think he might be your serial killer."

"Let's just say he's a person of interest."

"Well, you better go see about Harry," the agent says nonchalantly.

"Harry?" Tara says surprised.

"I take it that you haven't been to your division yet. They probably have him in interrogation as we speak. I'll jump on Mr. Wade this morning and have something for you ASAP."

Tara, baffled at the news about Harry, makes a beeline to Division. Harry Thornton is a vagrant in his mid-fifties and La Flore is one of many cities within his sizable territory. A few uniformed officers and detectives from the LFPD know Harry, but Tara knows him best. She has known him for years. A fly on the wall, he has proven to be a reliable informant, helping her on a number of cases. She attests that he can be belligerent and go off on tangents, quoting scripture when under the influence of cheap booze. He has his quirks and occasionally has had encounters with the law for homeless infractions. At over six feet tall with a menacing face, at times, he can be scary. Tara cannot imagine him involved in this degree of violence. Yes, he can be odd and yes, he can be troublesome, but hardly dangerous.

About ten minutes later, Tara approaches the three interrogation rooms and sees the "Interrogation in Session" light illuminated over one of the rooms. She quietly enters the observation room finding Commander Johnson peering through a large one-way window.

"Hey, Commander," Tara says.

She sits in a metal chair next to him gazing at the scruffy man sitting at a table oblivious to their presence. She instantly recognizes the longhaired man as Harry.

"We're about ten minutes into it," he tells her.

"Why is he here?" Tara asks, her curiosity now fever pitch.

"We found an incriminating item on him after we picked him up for public intoxication and harassment late last night. The item is a pair of women's underwear. We think they may belong to Kelly Vogel. I had Agent Sumner run DNA tests throughout the night. We should be getting something from him soon. Look, I am just as confused about this as you are. I know this isn't Harry's MO, but under the circumstances, I can't ignore this."

Her logic cannot help but concur with the commander. Tara knows, in her line of work, she must align herself with unscrupulous folks, i.e. Harry.

Harry, her mind asks intently as she chooses to stay on the sideline to see how events play out. *What the hell have you gotten yourself into?*

In the interrogation room, Detective Cummins is at his wits end.

"Harry, you know that I know that is your backpack we confiscated. Hell, you've had it as long as I've known you. In a glance, I can pick that thing out from a hundred backpacks. Yep, that's Harry's backpack. At some point, we're going to have to talk about the item we found."

Harry remains silent, unwilling to budge.

As Tara and the chief look on, Agent Sumner and Detective McVey enter the observation room. Tara and Agent Sumner stare at each other for a moment. She can tell the news he has is not good.

"What have you got for me, Agent?" the commander asks.

"Tests results show the underwear found in Harry's backpack belongs to Kelly Vogel."

There is a pause as Agent Sumner and Tara stare at each other once again.

"Go on," the commander says, anxious to hear the rest of the results.

"The semen found on Kelly Vogel, belongs to Harry."

Agent Sumner looks at Tara as if to apologize. Johnson gives Detective McVey a nod and he enters the interrogation room with Detective Cummins. Agent Sumner's departure leaves the commander and Tara sitting in the observation room. He turns his head slightly towards her.

"Sorry, Kiddo," he says in a low tone.

"Yeah," she responds, wearing a stoic face. Tara remains motionless and acutely focused on the episode unfolding before her.

Inside the interrogation room, "Detective Cummins, can I see you for a second?"

Cummins walks over and McVey whispers the tests results. Afterwards, they both stare at the vagrant sitting at the table. "Harry," Cummins says with a smile and "gotcha" look. "It's time to talk about that item, friend."

"Is my backpack ok? Where's my backpack?" Harry says in a grungy voice displaying missing teeth.

"You're backpack is fine, Harry. We're taking good care of it. This is Detective McVey. He's going to join us this morning."

"Hey, Harry." McVey holds out his hand and Harry cautiously engages in a handshake. McVey sits down and places a folder on the rectangular table. He opens the folder, revealing the photos of Kelly Vogel and slides them in front of Harry. The detectives remain silent observing his reaction. They can see the photos have an effect since he can barely glance at them before instantly looking away.

"Harry, I'm not going to beat around the bush on this," Cummins says calmly. "DNA test results show the underwear we found in your backpack belonged to this woman. Even worse, we found semen on the woman, Harry, and guess whose it is?"

The vagrant fidgets in his chair.

"Harry, you ok? Do you need something to drink?" McVey asks. Harry nods his head nervously. "I'll get you some water, is that ok?"

"Yeah, water's fine," he answers, realizing he is between a rock and a hard place. McVey returns with a bottle of water. Cummins and McVey look at each other as they notice the bottle quiver in his large trembling hands.

"Harry, I'm going to ask you some direct questions and I need you to be truthful. All we want is the truth."

Cummins leans over the table with his eyes locked on Harry.

"Did you kill this woman?"

"No, no I didn't kill anybody, honest," he answers.

"Harry, this is important. Do you know who did?"

"No, I don't. I swear I'm telling the truth."

Cummins sits back in his chair then looks over at McVey.

"Harry?" McVey weighs in. "Tell us how you acquired Kelly Vogel's underwear and how did your semen get on her body?" There is a long silence. Harry stares at his worn hands, holding the water bottle.

"Harry, we're not here to judge you. We just want the truth."

"I...I was walking from Claremore on Old Highway 77. I went off in the bushes to take a leak. I was taking a leak when I saw something lying in a clearing. At first, I thought it was a deer that been hit by a car. I thought if it were fresh enough maybe, I might have something to eat. When I walked to it, I found it was the woman in that picture, but she was already dead, already dead. I didn't do nothing," Harry says, his voice starting to sound frantic.

"Alright Harry, settle down, you're doing great," McVey says. "You found her already dead, what happened next?"

What happened next has Harry reluctant to share with the detectives. He feels if they have not judged him now, they will after this.

"Harry, what happened next?" Cummins interjects with a calm persuasion.

Harry looks up to see the two detectives staring at him like parents, waiting to hear what they already know. Unbeknownst to him, Tara and Commander Johnson share the same look behind the one-way glass.

"This is important Harry. I wouldn't ask you if it wasn't."

Harry looks nervously down at his hands.

"I saw this naked woman on the ground. It...it had been a long time since I seen a naked woman as pretty as her. At first I didn't do anything, but then I saw her underwear."

"Where were they?" Cummins asks.

"Like two, three feet away. I went and picked them up...and...and I...smelled them. After I did that, I couldn't help it. I relieved myself on her."

"Meaning you masturbated on her?" McVey says.

"Yeah, that's what I did," Harry responds, clearly embarrassed.

"So, you did your deed and kept the underwear. Is that it, Harry?" McVey asks.

"That's it," Harry responds blushing heavily.

"Harry, why didn't you contact us?" Cummins asks.

"I was afraid you'd think I killed her. After I'd done what I did, I was afraid you'd think I was some sort of a sick perv or something."

The trio remained silent, absorbing the events of the interrogation.

"Detective Tanner is going to hear about this…isn't she?"

The detectives glance at each other.

"Harry, you did very well this morning and you have been a big help to us," Cummins says. The two detectives rise from their seats. "We'll be right back."

Upon entering the observation room, "Ok, Harry is one sick puppy, but if he killed Kelly Vogel, then I'm Elvis," Cummins blurts.

"Thank you for that brilliant assessment, Detective," the commander responds. "Ok, on one hand, there is a consensus among us that Harry didn't kill Kelly Vogel. In five murders, our killer hasn't left as much as a molecule and Harry's got DNA all over the place," the commander says.

"Good point," McVey adds.

"On the other hand, he couldn't give us anything that could really help us." Johnson leans back in his chair and runs both hands slowly down his face, letting his large hands fall into his lap.

"What's the call, Commander?" Cummins asks.

Johnson looks around at the three agents.

"In light of the physical evidence we found on Harry and the fact that he got nabbed for public drunkenness and harassment, we're going to hold him in custody because right now he's all we've got," the commander says.

"Who knows, maybe he might remember something that can help us," McVey adds.

Commander Johnson also knows that detaining Harry as a suspect will take some of the heat off of LFPD, Chief Nirez and Mayor Saks...for now. Tara feels the vibration of her phone against her hip.

She sees the call is from Investigation Division. She quickly gathers her belongings and springs from her chair.

"Gentlemen, I have to go."

"That's rather obvious," Cummins says.

"Do you have anything for me, Commander?"

"Not at the moment," Johnson says, finding Tara's sudden change in disposition peculiar.

Moments later, Tara looks for a quiet and secluded place to talk. She heads to the first empty interrogation room. There, she retrieves her phone and presses the return dial button. After a short wait, "Agent Jenkins," a voice comes from her cell phone.

"Agent Jenkins, this is Detective Tanner. What have you got for me?"

CHAPTER 14

Fit To Kill

Agent Jenkins dictates her information on Tara's suspect. "Daniel S. Wade. You won't believe what the "S" stands for," the agent says.

"What?" Tara asks.

"Strange."

"Strange? That's such an odd name, no pun intended."

"You ever heard of Robert McNamara?" the agent asks.

"The name rings a bell, but I can't put my finger on it."

"He's the former Secretary of Defense under Presidents Kennedy and Johnson. Well, his middle name was Strange. I'm guessing his parents were probably fans of his." The agent continues with her list.

"Born June 6, 1967 in Tacoma, Washington, Six feet, 190 pounds, brown hair, hazel eyes, never married, resides at 824 Mitchell Road in the Tomlinson District. It's a secluded but nice neighborhood on the outskirts of town on La Flore's west side. I've been there a couple of times to visit my in-laws," the agent says fondly. "Parents were James and Sharon Wade, both deceased. He's the only child, no juvenile record. Faith is agnostic, joined the Navy in July of eighty-five, no disciplinary action against him, but this is interesting."

"What's that?" Tara asks.

"He washed out of *SEAL* school while ranked third in his class, one week before graduating."

"That is interesting," Tara responds. "Does it say why he washed out?"

"That's even more peculiar. His records merely state for…psychological reasons."

Tara weighs in on Agent Jenkins last words. "Psychological reasons," she says lost in thought.

"What are you thinking, Detective?"

"I'm thinking if Mr. Wade is our killer. He may not have any motives. Maybe he just snapped."

"Maybe. I've also got a feeling there is more to this than his records indicate," the agent says shrewdly.

"What else have you got?"

"He left the Navy in ninety-five, lived in San Diego for six months and moved to La Flore."

"So, he's lived here about fourteen years." Tara concludes.

"Looks like he worked some of the local gyms as a personal trainer; in ninety-eight he applied for a city LLC business license under Fit Now Private Personal Training; he's got a private training studio on the west side by Baker Brothers BMW."

"I know where that is," Tara says.

"His tax return from last year reported his personal earnings at $98,000. You'd have to be making at least that much to operate in that area," the agent says.

"It's amazing how much a trainer can make with the right clientele even in a trainer-saturated city like La Flore," Tara thinks to herself.

"As for Daniel's criminal history,"

"I was beginning to wonder when you were going to get to that," Tara interrupts.

"Sorry to rain on your parade, but Mr. Wade has nothing to raise suspicions for criminal activity, not to mention serial murder. He has a couple of traffic violations. That's it."

Tara ponders for a moment. "I've got a suspect who doesn't have the juvenile or criminal background that would give him the propensity to commit five heinous murders; is that correct?"

"That's correct," the agent responds.

"But, going through SEAL training would give him the abilities to do what our killer's doing," Tara concludes.

"I'll put it to you like this, I dated a guy years back that washed out midway through SEAL school and he was an accomplished decathlete in college, I mean this guy was a rock. At a week from graduating, you've completed the SEAL course and the top five at that point are a unique set of individuals. I believe Mr. Wade was one of those individuals. As far as his abilities go, if he's the type of trainer who leads by example, and being a high end trainer in La Flore indicates that he is, there's no doubt in my mind…Daniel Wade is definitely fit to kill."

Tara feels reassurance from Agent Jenkins words, since they run parallel with her thoughts.

"The psychological part, causing a shoe-in graduate who was third in his class to wash out a week before graduating definitely makes your guy a person worth looking into. I've emailed the information to you along with his latest DMV photo."

There is brief silence, then, "Hey, Jenkins, why didn't you take the Feds offer?" Tara asks, referring to the agent declining an offer to work for the FBI. Agent Jenkins knows Tara's question is a compliment rather than an inquiry.

"I love what I'm doing and where I'm at," the agent responds. "Besides, look who's asking," she rebuts with a compliment of her own.

"Thank you for the info, Agent Jenkins. Once again, you have come through for me big time. Oh, wait a minute," Tara says as a thought comes to mind.

"I need you to check out something else for me."

"That was quick," the agent responds. "What is it?"

"Chief Nirez mentioned something a while back about a killer using proxies for victims," Tara says, not knowing whether what she is saying made any sense. "Do you know anything about such a case?"

"No, I don't, but it sounds interesting," the Agent responds. "I'll check out the Chief's records and see what comes up, but this might take a while."

Tara, knowing Agent Jenkins is one of only two people in the entire city with a high enough security clearance to review records on high-ranking officials, feels even more privileged having her as a colleague.

"Do you need me to get more information on the case?" Tara asks.

"No. Besides, it takes the fun out of the hunt," the agent says welcoming the challenge.

"Thanks again," Tara responds graciously.

"Good luck, Detective and…be careful."

Tara senses the second part of Agent Jenkins statement was far more earnest than the first.

Moments later, she walks out of the interrogation room and is surprised to see Detective McVey in the hallway casually leaning against the wall. Her expression asks him why is he there.

"I heard your voice," he replies. "I couldn't make out what was being said, so you're safe."

"That was an excellent job on the interrogation this morning," she says walking by McVey.

"Detective, do you have a minute?"

Tara stops and faces him. "Sure," she replies nonchalantly.

"I...I don't know if you remember our confrontation at Pathology."

"How could I forget," Tara remarks. "Look...it's ok. As far as I'm concerned, the matter is settled."

"I'm really glad to hear that, but this is something I really need to get off my chest."

Tara, though a little intrigued, is a bit apprehensive about what is about to be said.

"Ok, let's hear it."

"That day, was my anniversary. Well, it would have been my anniversary."

"How long has it been since your divorce, Detective McVey?" she asks sympathetically, and on an intuitive guess.

"Going on three years," he says with a heavy sigh. "On my fifth tour she couldn't take anymore."

Tara, moved by McVey's confession is curious as to what this has to do with her.

"The thing is, I volunteered for a fifth after four consecutive tours in Iraq. Can you believe that? I could have gone home to my wife and kids, but I had to be hardcore, gung ho." He chuckles slightly, in rctrospect. "It got me the Navy Cross, but it cost me much more."

McVey pulls out his cell phone and shuffles through pictures. He stops at one and hands the phone to Tara. "There she is. Her name is Tammy."

Tara looks at the stunning blonde on the screen.

I can't see it, but apparently, there's enough resemblance between us for McVey, her mind asserts.

"She's from Leesburg, Georgia," he says.

Well, being a southern girl, that might be a game changer, she thinks again.

"I saw Tammy in you that day in Pathology. My head was not right, not right at all. You know the real tragedy in this, Detective?"

"What's that?"

"The bitterness I feel at times isn't directed at Tammy. Hell, I don't blame her for what she did. The bitterness I feel is at me for being so damn stupid and selfish."

Tara remained silent as she felt McVey having a moment.

"How do you feel?" she asks calmly.

"I...I feel like I've finally gotten a huge weight off my chest."

"I'm glad to have been of help and I appreciate you letting me in on your story. I hope things work out for you. In the meantime, we have a killer to catch." Her last words hit home with McVey.

"Yes. We do."

Later that day, Tara sits at her desk, honed in on her computer screen. She thoroughly goes through her copious amount of email thoroughly as if looking for a present. Finally, Tara sees "Intelligence Division/Daniel Wade". She sees the attachment icon that contains the photo, clicks it and reclines in her chair as it downloads. The wait feels like an eternity when the DMV photo finally appears on her screen. The photo is a head shot that exposes Daniel's shoulders and upper chest. He wears a red polo shirt and a pleasant look on a lean face.

Tara's natural impulse is to compare Daniel to her trainer, Frank. Daniel is far from an unattractive man, wearing his forties better than most. Compared to the male model features of Frank however, there is no comparison. The photo also suggests that Daniel is just as lean and muscular as Frank, who on his fattest day stays around seven percent body fat, but Daniel does not fill his six-foot frame nearly as well.

Given the heinous nature of the crimes, Tara does not sense from the photo that Daniel Wade could be the harbinger of death that has the residents of La Flore living in fear. He is also not what she'd envisioned as she thinks back to the conversation earlier with Agent Jenkins about SEALS.

"Looks can be deceiving," she thinks, paraphrasing Frank. Tara knows she has to get up close and personal with Mr. Wade. "That's how I will truly know," she says with confidence. Unlike the Sexton case, where she had to deal with the devastating loss of her father, Tara's head is now clear, and her heart now free from grief.

At twilight, Tara heads to Frank's studio. Wanting to see if he may know something about Daniel Wade, it gives her a reason for a pleasant surprise visit. She arrives at the studio and walks inside. Her tunnel vision on Daniel Wade makes her oblivious to the empty training floor and the subtle sounds emanating from Frank's office. The door repels her, as she is surprised to find it locked.

"Frank, it's Tara."

The commotion is instantaneous and Tara quickly realizes what is happening.

"Open the door, Frank," she says in a calm yet assertive voice.

She keeps her composure while experiencing an adrenaline rush. Time passes before there is movement on the doorknob.

When the door opens, she finds Frank standing in the doorway, his clothes rumpled, and with a look on his face, guilty as sin. She does not enter the office. Nevertheless, the smell of sex is stifling. Standing next to Frank's desk is a very attractive, well-toned shirtless young man. Tara stares at the young man whose streamlined physique has model qualities. She turns her attention to Frank, who cannot look her in the face.

"I came to find out about a trainer named Daniel Wade. I thought maybe you might know something; maybe I should have called first," she says in a somber voice.

"Sorry... I don't know him, and maybe you should have," he says, still reluctant to meet her gaze.

"Ok...I guess I'll see you around...Sorry if I interrupted you and your...friend."

The drive home under the night sky finds Tara clearly upset. Her phone rings and Tara checks the incoming number. For the fourth time Frank's number appears on her screen and for the fourth time...she does not answer.

Vivid flashes mixed with passionate sounds of her mother and dark haired lover engaging in torrid sex roam her thoughts. The flashes soon morph into visions of her and the young lover, then her and Frank, then her mother and Frank, and on, and on.

Tara's rational mind tries to override the carnal melee running amok in her head to avoid an emotional hurricane. She knows this turn of events pales compared to the loss of her father, but knowing what she is about to face, Tara recognizes she cannot be off her mental game when she meets her suspect.

This can't be another Sexton case, echoes in her head.

"Why am I upset in the first place?" Tara asks herself aloud. "He's not my husband. Hell, he's not even straight."

The unusual pitch of her voice during her last statement strikes an amusing chord and stirs something deep inside her. As it surfaces, a grin takes hold of her face. It soon progresses to a giggle. Before long, she is engaged in full-blown laughter. "Oh, Tara," she exclaims between bouts. "You're too much." She spoofs her intuitive gift, once again failing her in matters of the heart. "Of all the hot men in La Flore you'd have as a lover, you choose a gay one. Can you pick 'em or what?"

CHAPTER 15

Shopping for a Trainer

"*I* couldn't quite put my finger on it then, with the excitement and all...but we know the real Frank now don't we, child," says the soft southern drawl. *Tara finds herself in a vast and dark space, standing before the reflective barrier. A clear image of her mother wearing only a white silk slip reflects radiantly off its surface.*

"He was right you know. Things are not at times, as they seem. Deep down, you suspected there was something about Frank. Your dream about him and me would not have turned out the way it did if you hadn't. Once again, your intuitive gift let you down when it comes to matters of the heart. I know you had feelings for Frank, but don't fret that, Tara," she says dotingly. "Your heart did not forsake you with Dale."

"Don't think for a second this will get you off the hook, Momma," Tara snaps. "Just be thankful Daddy insisted I called you Momma instead of Rosa Faye."

Tara's mother sighs and shakes her head. "I gave up on being reconciled with you years ago," she says. "The fact is, I was a broken bird long before I met your daddy, and deep down, I strongly suspect you know that. He knew exactly what he was getting into when he married me. What you don't realize is that he was broken too. We were two broken souls in a broken place with a broken future. We were perfect for each other, so it seemed. He'd use my philandering as an excuse to drink till he was unconscious and I'd use his drinking as an excuse to have my way with as many as men I wanted. Then came you."

Tara's mother gets an incredulous look from her daughter. "Oh yes, Tara, you are your daddy's child. There are some things a mother just knows and besides...we weren't broken in that way. You are the only reason we decided to move to La Flore. Back home, we had no future. Your daddy and I sadly had accepted it. Your future, on the other hand, changed everything and despite all the bad you saw, your daddy and I loved each other very much. It was a dysfunctional marriage, but we lived up to our promise, till death do us part. You've done a miraculous thing, Tara. You have broken a tragic cycle that I, my mother, her mother, and a long line of our women-folk couldn't. If you'd lived in my time and place, maybe you'd understand."

For the first time for as long as she can remember, Tara is acutely attentive to her mother's words.

"You've paved a bright future for Sara and Megan and you won't find a better man than the one lying next to you. Don't fret over Frank, because you need your head and heart clear...to face him."

Tara's mother looks away and gestures with her head. As Tara's sight follows, she sees the dark figure standing a few feet away.

From the onset, she sees a stark contrast from her previous encounter. The figure is no longer a mere shadow but now has vague features. Tara instantly hones in on the features of the face, but they are too obscure to make out.

***

The piercing sound of the alarm awakens her. Instinctively, she reaches to her nightstand and without looking, hits the snooze button with skillful precision. Groggy, she lays back and stares at the blank ceiling. She looks over to find Dale still asleep.

"I know I have a good man, Momma," she says softly under her breath. "I know."

Later that morning, Tara is on the phone at her desk.

"Fit Now Personal Training, this is Becky; how I can help you?" says the voice of the receptionist.

"Hi, my name is Tara and I'm inquiring about your services."

The receptionist, who sounds in her mid-twenties, starts her pitch. After what transpired last night at Frank's studio, Tara finds herself precariously straddling between investigating a possible suspect for serial murder and shopping for a new trainer while listening to the well-rehearsed pitch.

"Can you tell me a little about the trainers there," she asks.

"Well, there's only one trainer and he's the owner. His name is Daniel Wade. He has been training in La Flore for fourteen years. He holds four training certifications and clients love him. He's really a super guy."

Tara senses the sincerity in Becky's voice.

"Would you like to schedule a consultation?"

"Yes, I would," Tara replies. "How soon can I come in?"

"He's booked till three and he doesn't train clients after three."

"He doesn't train clients after three?" Tara asks, slightly astonished. "What are his hours?"

"Daniels hours are from six a.m. till three p.m. He has an opening tomorrow at three. I can put you in…Is that ok?"

"Yes that's fine, Becky."

"I'm putting you on the schedule now and…it's done. I'm looking forward to seeing you tomorrow at three o'clock, Tara. If you want to get more acquainted with us before you arrive, here's our web address."

Tara writes down the website.

"Thanks, Becky and I'm looking forward to seeing you."

When Tara hangs up, her mind ponders two things that immediately come to mind, Becky's disposition and Daniel Wade's hours.

Becky really seems happy working there, and she has a very high regard for Mr. Wade. I sensed no duress at all, she asserts. If Mr. Wade is in fact our serial killer, then Becky is either too terrified to expose him, oblivious to what's going on, or is his accomplice. Based on our phone conversation,

I've already crossed out the first possibility. She thinks about Daniel Wade's hours. I'm no expert on the lives of personal trainers. I do know Frank makes good money and it is common for him to be at his studio from sun up til sun down. If Mr. Wade works the hours his receptionist described, then he could have the time to commit the murders.

Tara takes time to look at the big picture. After playing devil's advocate with herself, she finds some things hard to swallow.

He's still got too much on his plate, running a successful training business and engaging in serial murder without leaving a trace? These murders took time and planning and despite his hours, I see a very tight timeline that would leave him practically no room for error. It would take extraordinary abilities to pull it off under his circumstances.

Tara recalls her conversation with Agent Jenkins, reminding her who she may be dealing with.

The top five at that point are a very unique set of individuals. I believe Mr. Wade was one of those individuals.

Tara logs onto "Fit Now's" website. She rummages through the site's pages spending most of her time reading client testimonials and bios.

"Detective Tanner," she hears the voice of Commander Johnson as he walks to his office. He gestures her to follow him. Upon entering, "Close the door and have a seat," he says. Remembering her sudden exit during Harry's interrogation, Tara has a strong hunch where this is heading.

"Tell me your hightailing it out of an interrogation has something to do with a suspect," he says while his large hands skillfully rip the skin off an orange.

"Yes, a possible suspect, Commander," she replies.

She reveals her case to Johnson, starting with the comment about proxy killings made by Chief Nirez, the resemblance her daughter Megan saw between victim Penny Keester and their neighbor Faye Woodard, the background check on her alleged suspect and her illuminating conversation on Navy SEALs with Agent Jenkins. When she's finished, a pile of skin on the commander's desk is all that remains of the orange he swiftly devoured.

"Not to dismiss anything, but to the best of my knowledge, I haven't heard of a case like that since it happened, and didn't think I ever would," the commander says.

"Mr. Wade has no criminal history and he's a successful personal trainer. Personal trainers are like clergy in this city you know," he says while sitting back in his chair. "Well, it's a good thing it's not my wife's trainer, or there'd be hell to pay." Tara finds humor in his last comment but feels to some degree, he was being serious. "The SEAL background and the psych profile on this suspect are something worth looking at. When is your interview with him?"

"Tomorrow at three p.m."

"I know you like working alone to use your mojo, Kiddo, but you might need some backup on this one."

"It's at his studio in plain sight, Commander. I'll be fine, really. After a moment, "How's Harry?" she asks.

"I don't know how Harry is, but I do know the DA wants to move forward ASAP and I don't know how much longer I can stall him," the commander says.

La Flore's DA, Kenneth James, is talented, hardnosed and ambitious, with the skills and cunning to make almost any legal allegation stick. Worse, he is a close associate of Democratic Mayoral candidate Eddie Lamar.

"I'll keep you posted," she says, feeling his sense of urgency. As Tara walks to the door, she hears low laughter from the commander. She turns, puzzled by his bizarre behavior. "Commander?" she asks.

"Ah, I was just thinking, a personal trainer that's a serial killer, in La Flore…who'd think of something that absurd?"

"I know," Tara responds looking back at the commander, "Sounds like something out of a book."

Forty minutes later, "After hearing about my interrogation, I didn't think you'd ever want to see me again," Harry says, sitting at a table wearing an orange inmate's jumpsuit. "I figured you'd think I was some sort of sick pervert…a monster."

Tara sits across the table, wearing a pleasant expression while reading the body language of her long time acquaintance. She can clearly see how embarrassed he is since he feels she knows about what he had done to victim Kelly Vogel.

"How are you doing, Harry?" Tara asks, trying to defuse his discomfort.

"I don't like it here," he says sadly. "They took away my backpack and people aren't very nice in here."

"Yeah, it kinda sucks doesn't it?"

"I didn't kill that woman. You gotta believe me. I need you to help me get out of here," Harry says with a hint of desperation in his voice.

"I believe you, Harry," she asserts. "Trust me, I will help you get out of here and will make sure you get your backpack, ok?"

"Why did you wait so long to come and see me?" he asks. "Is it because of what I'd done to that woman?" Harry caught Tara off guard with his question.

"No...no, no that's not it at all," she responds, a bit startled. "I'm trying to catch a killer and one of the victims happens to be Kelly Vogel."

He sits back in his chair and crosses his arms. "I guess your killer's not being very cooperative," he murmurs in a low tone.

"No, Harry, not at all. That's why if you remember anything that could be of help, you must tell me, ok? You still know how to get in contact with me?"

Harry nods his head in affirmatively.

"Good." Tara takes a moment to look into the eyes of a man who despite his outward appearance and the perverted act he had committed, she knows is innocent without a doubt.

"Hey, Harry, I have to go."

"You'll come visit me again?" he asks, glad to know Tara had not passed any negative judgment on him.

"Of course I will," she responds, as if the question needed asking.

As she watches the sad scene of jailers escorting Harry back to his cell. Her pleasant expression vanishes. Tara does not think about her upcoming interview with the alleged suspect. At this moment, she wants nothing more than to see Harry a free man again, with his beloved backpack.

CHAPTER 16

On His Turf

There is an eeriness in the drive as Tara weaves through the midafternoon traffic towards La Flore's west side. She recalls the day she met with Chief Nirez in her commander's office and the events afterwards at her desk. Tara remembers asking herself out of frustration, *Would I know you if I saw you?* She ponders the thought.

Becky adores him and his clients seem to as well. I know my neighbor, Faye, sure does. I have a feeling they have not seen the other Daniel Wade, and it is unlikely he is just going to introduce that side of himself to me either. Prolific serial killers are accomplished chameleons, and if Mr. Wade is our killer, he's no different.

Tara feels apprehension since her nose for sensing bad souls might not work on Daniel Wade as well as she hopes. "No," she says in an assertive outburst. "I'm going on his turf and I'm going alone because that's where he's more likely to show his other self." There is a moment of silence…then, "All I have to do is provoke him."

Arriving at the lush west side business district, Tara realizes how volatile and risky this endeavor could become. By provoking Daniel Wade, she may endanger the life of someone else. She strongly suspects Penny Keester was a proxy victim for her neighbor Faye Woodard. "Apparently, Mr. Wade didn't take kindly to Faye's weight gain," Tara thinks aloud. Suddenly, a thought hits her, forcing her to pull over abruptly in a minor panic.

Sara, her mind screams. Often mistaken for sisters, Tara sees her daughter as her perfect proxy.

A late model Mercedes pulls up next to her and its passenger window rolls down. "Miss, Miss?" asks a middle-aged man, who saw Tara's abrupt maneuver. She rolls down her window sensing the man's concern.

"Miss, are you ok?" he asks.

"Yes, I'm fine…Thank you." Tara responds with a smile and hand wave to show she is all right and to express her gratitude. The Mercedes cruises off. After a few minutes, she regains her composure.

"If I do this, there's a possibility I could be endangering my daughter's life," she asserts in earnest. Tara can see the Baker Brothers BMW sign off in the distance. Despite her disturbing thoughts about Sara, she is compelled to continue. Tara drives with her sight fixed on the dealership sign until she is able to see the adjacent buildings. Immediately, she spots her destination next to the small dealership. Her eyes lock on the sign that reads, "Fit Now Private Personal Training."

Tara parks in front of the building and sits for a moment. She looks at the time on her phone to see that she has twenty minutes until her appointment. Not wanting to arrive too early, she sits in her car, observing the building. The structure seemed abandoned even with several cars parked in front of it. In a strange twist, Tara does something she never has prior to an interview. She checks her weapon before exiting the car. Strolling the short distance to the studio, she feels a slight knot in her stomach.

Upon entering the small waiting area, she recognizes Becky at once from her photo on the website. She cannot ignore the rich sounds of Aerosmith and an intense session emanating from the training floor. Becky is sitting at the front desk, on a plush stool, in the midst of a phone conversation.

"We really don't do super, super slow here ma'am," she responds, perplexed by the inquiry. Becky and Tara immediately connect and exchange puzzled looks at each other.

"I know of super slow but not super, super slow. Are you sure you're not mistaken ma'am?" Becky and Tara find the humor in Becky's remark.

"Oh, you've done it with a trainer in San Francisco?" They both look at each other mildly astonished by the news. "Well, I'm sorry I couldn't be of help and I hope you find what you're looking for…Bye."

"What was that all about?" Tara asks.

"I don't know," Becky responds shaking her head. "In this business, you get requests for all types of training methods. I take it you're Tara," Becky says in a warm and friendly tone. The redhead extends her hand to greet her.

"Yes, I am," Tara replies as the two shake hands.

"So, where in the south are you from?" the receptionist asks. "I picked it up during our last phone call."

"Alabama…Hueytown to be exact," Tara replies.

"I have cousins in South Carolina and trust me, you sound nothing like them," Becky says assuredly. Tara is captivated listening to the training session that sounds more like unbridled sex.

"Oh, that's Dan and Wanda going at it. They can get a bit carried away, if you know what I mean. Did you want to do a health assessment today or just a consultation?"

"The consultation will be fine," Tara replies.

"Well, you still have ten minutes, so please have a seat. Dan will be with you shortly." Tara sits while Becky preps for closing.

As she waits, the training between Daniel and Wanda continues to draw her undivided attention. The intensity, passion and erotic energies between the pair have Tara empathizing with Wanda. Despite the agony she appears to be experiencing, Tara knows Wanda is having the time of her life. She begins to reminisce about her past sessions with Frank and the same passionate energies they shared.

"How's your stress level?" Frank asks

"What stress level?" she replies, totally exhausted.

Tara becomes lost in emotion. Hearing Daniel and Wanda, she realizes how much she will miss training and being with Frank; how much she will miss looking forward to his firm eager embrace. Her heart is heavy and her mind cloudy.

"Tara, are you ok? You look a bit flushed."

"Yes, I'm fine, thank you. Where's your water fountain?"

"The cooler is right next to you," Becky responds.

"Oh, yes...so it is," Tara says to her chagrin. After drinking two cups from the cooler, Tara feels her thoughts of Frank have gotten out of hand. She looks at the wall clock to see that it is one minute until three and Daniel and Wanda's training session has already ended. Her mind screams, *I've got to get out of this tailspin...now!*

Suddenly, the door from the training floor opens and Wanda emerges drenched in sweat.

"Did you have a good one?" Becky asks, with a sly grin.

"When don't I have a good one?" Wanda replies. "It could have been better if it were a leg day, but what the hell...It is what it is."

"Wanda, this is Tara," Becky says introducing the two. "Tara, the loud one here, who's stuck on Aerosmith, is Wanda."

"Loud? Give me a young stud and I'll show you loud," Wanda says boldly. "As for Aerosmith, I'm weak. What can I say…deal with it."

Tara is amused at the boorish camaraderie between Wanda and Becky. She stands as Wanda approaches and gives her an energetic handshake while drying off with a towel.

"Glad to meet you, Tara."

"Likewise," Tara replies.

Tara notices Becky disappear towards the training floor.

"Welcome aboard, and I sure hope you like training hard," Wanda says.

"Thank you, and as a matter of fact…I do."

Wanda leaves the studio and Tara feels she has finally recovered from her breakdown. She gets her bearings when Becky reappears.

"Tara…Dan is ready to see you."

CHAPTER 17

The Appointment

"He's in his office," Becky says.

Tara finds her way to Daniel's office. She arrives to find a figure leaning casually against the front of a desk, with muscular arms crossed over a lean chest.

"Hello, Tara. I'm Daniel," he says in a voice deeper than she had anticipated. He flashes a bright smile and reaches his hand out to welcome her.

"Daniel, would you prefer Daniel or Dan?"

"Becky is really the only person that calls me Dan. I prefer Daniel," he replies.

As she reaches out her hand to reciprocate, she sees the man in front of her is clearly not the person she saw in the DMV photo. *"The photo didn't do him justice,"* she concludes.

"Excuse me," Becky interrupts. "Dan, do you need anything from me before I go?"

"No, Becky and thanks for fixing that glitch in the schedule earlier, you're the best."

"I know," Becky responds. "Bye, Tara and hope we see more of you."

"Bye, Becky." Tara says, in a friendly tone, realizing she and Daniel are now completely alone. She instantly feels his commanding presence and despite his awkward polite demeanor, her senses now go on high alert. For a man in his forties, he is definitely in the elite class of his peers, not to mention men of any other age group. As the two engage in a firm handshake, Tara is convinced Daniel has the physical prowess to pull off La Flore's killings. Something that jumps out at her is how immaculate and meticulous his studio appears.

"Is your place always this clean? I mean this is really impressive," she says.

"Well, Tara, as they say, cleanliness is next to Godliness," Daniel responds, attempting to mix humor and sarcasm.

"They also say a clean desk is the sign of a sick mind," Tara says, attempting to do the same.

Tara can clearly see how if Daniel is La Flore's killer, he could murder and not leave a trace. She senses that it is time to get down to business...It is time to open Pandora's Box and get a glimpse of the other Daniel Wade.

"I'm sorry, Tara, have a seat." Tara sits in a comfortable office chair with her legs crossed and Daniel perches on top of his desk.

"Why are you here?" he asks shrewdly. "I'm getting the impression that it's not for my services. You look fantastic and I would not be surprised if you already have a trainer. I will tell you that I don't do solicitations. So if you're here to sell me something, I'm not interested."

"Daniel, I'm a detective with the LFPD and I'm investigating a series of murders throughout the city over the past few months."

Launching her attack, she focuses on Daniel's body language. Tara knows the timing was perfect. She catches him completely off guard and hopes he will not be able to control involuntary impulses. Her strategy pays off as Daniel's fair skin, for half an instant, becomes flushed. Daniel finds himself in a precarious position. Feeling the flash of heat on his skin, he knows that he compromised himself. The question on his mind is whether Tara saw it.

He sees Tara sitting casually in her chair, wearing a poker face. Daniel knows an ambush when he sees it and realizes he is suddenly a victim of one. "So, Tara...or is it Detective now?" he asks.

"I'm going to leave that entirely up to you. Look, you are not being accused of anything."

"Oh, really," he counters, now slightly agitated.

"If you'd let me finish, I'll explain. Because of your background and psychological profile," Tara continues her monologue and can plainly see the psychological profile part hit a nerve, further agitating him. "You, along with a list of others, are deemed persons of interest. That's all."

Daniel calms down believing that he is not an isolated target.

"So, Detective, what do you want from me?"

"Well for starters, I want to know where you were, what you were doing and who you were with on Thursday, the sixth of this month, between seven-thirty p.m. and one o'clock a.m."

"Detective, my days…my life is pretty regimented."

"I'm sure it is, Daniel, but I'm not interested in a tangent about your personal life. I just want you to answer the question."

"Ok," he says, wearing his frustration on his face. "I was at home…alone…watched an episode of Biggest Loser, fixed my meals for the next day, went to bed around ten-thirty and no, Detective, there is no one who can verify it." He pauses for a moment, and then looks Tara squarely in the face. "Come to think of it, last I heard, LFPD had a suspect in custody," he taunts. "Isn't that correct?"

Tara sees the opportunity to do what she had come for… to provoke her suspect.

"Yes that's correct, a homeless vagrant and a frightening sight, but you want to know something? I feel I can tell you this, since it wouldn't bother someone who's innocent and all." Tara feels a strange shift of energy in the room that makes her hair follicles stand on end. She locks her dark eyes on Daniel's as she continues. "Even though most folks would rate the man in custody somewhere between a primate and a possum, he's a much higher species than the coward and scum committing these murders," Tara says with a hint of her mother's condescending tone.

She notices Daniel's face go blank and then snap back.

"Is there anything else I can help you with?" he asks in a calm yet disturbing manner.

"No...Yes," she catches herself. "When you see Becky, if you can refrain from portraying me as a complete bitch...I'd appreciate it."

Daniel answers her request with a subtle grin. "I'm sure I can manage that."

Tara rises out of her chair, straightening her clothes. "Thank you for your time and hopefully, you won't have to see me again." Daniel remains perched on his desk with a pleasant but deceptive smile. "I'll see myself out," she says with a calm assertion.

Tara realizes the short distance to the office door requires her to face away from him. She is uneasy since the energy she felt earlier persists. Tara walks to the door, trying not to appear nervous. She positions her handbag across her body for easier access to her weapon. As she steps through the office doorway, her heightened senses and law enforcement training could not protect her from the talon like grips that clutch her shoulders viciously, sucking her back into the office.

Before she realizes what has happened. Tara suddenly finds herself in the vise grip of an apex predator.

"Not so fast! You had your turn, Detective…Now it's mine."

Daniel quickly turns Tara to face him and introduces a crushing head butt on the bridge of her nose. The pain and blood from the blow is instant. Daniel releases his grip and Tara, dazed and in pain, staggers out of the office onto the training floor. She retrieves her Glock and fires two aimless shots before Daniel snatches the weapon away. Holding her shooting arm, he hyper-extends it at the elbow, resulting in a loud and violent snap. Daniel inflicts another heavy blow to the bridge of Tara's crushed and bloodied nose with his forearm, then sweeps her legs with a kick, sending her crashing to the floor. The unbearable pain renders her powerless. Her shooting arm dangles past the elbow as she rolls helplessly on the floor.

"Detective, you come to my studio and insult me. A clean desk is the sign of a sick mind? What are you saying? I have a sick mind because I like things clean?" Daniel kneels next to her, her face swelling rapidly.

"This time, I'm going to ask the questions, and I don't want to hear a tangent about your personal problems," he mocks sarcastically. "There are no other persons of interest, are there?"

Tara cannot reply since she is oblivious to everything but her excruciating pain.

"Answer the question, Detective." Getting no response, he palms her swollen face and presses firmly, making her squirm. "I take it, that's a no."

The thought on Daniel's mind takes him to an even darker place. "That can only mean one thing," he says in a tone that goes from disturbing to outright sinister. "Since there were never any...other persons of interest, and from the way you looked me in the eyes when you made your silly ass comment, I know, you were referring to me."

He stands and gives a heavy sigh, then looks down upon Tara, whose face has swollen beyond recognition.

"You honestly thought you could get away with this? That I would just let you walk away? No, no, I'm afraid I can't do that. I know it's not polite to kick a person when they're down, but I think in this case, I can make an exception. Oh yes...one more thing before I forget. In light of our little...time together, Becky will know you only as...the complete bitch."

Daniel turns on the stereo and cranks up the volume. Metal music engulfs the studio, muffling the horrific sounds of torture from the hail of bone crushing kicks to Tara's face and body.

CHAPTER 18

Daniel's Next Move

I've seen the killer's face, and I know his name; it's Daniel Wade.

Tara's mind hammers the thought while sitting in her car, already an hour into her stakeout. She is at least fifty yards from the training studio, but with the help of powerful binoculars, she has a clear view of the front entrance and the parking lot. The hour of surveillance allows her to rehash her earlier meeting with Daniel. Neither the flush of his skin or the eerie shift in energy, telling her that someone, or something, other than Daniel was in his office brings Tara to her resolute conclusion. It was the encounter Tara had after she walked out of his office, an encounter that seemed, ghostly.

Tara walks out of Daniel's office after their appointment. She passes the cardio area and notices an attractive woman strolling on a treadmill. She finds it odd since Daniel did not train clients after three and Becky had already left for the day. Seeing Tara, the woman eyes her with a friendly smile. Suddenly, time moves in slow motion as Tara looks into Thelma Carson's stare. She does not see a woman who looks stunning for sixty-one. Thelma's stare hurls Tara's thoughts back to the examination room with murder victim Kelly Vogel.

She feels the intense release of energy left by the victim's grieving husband, while looking upon the face of the deceased, lying on the examination table.

"Yes, yes…I see it. That woman is the one isn't she? You died for her didn't you?" Tara asked, looking at the victim as if to get an answer. Kelly's eyes open slowly and widen against a lifeless face displaying milky pupils. Then, tears begin to well and stream down her face.

Ten minutes into her stakeout, Tara observed Thelma leave the studio.

"This woman is able to come and go as she pleases. She has to be close to Daniel in some way."

Tara notices the woman does not have the pleasant demeanor she had seen earlier.

"It's not like she's angry or frightened, but more…disappointed," she tells herself. "Hmm, I get the feeling they may be lovers."

Tara watches through her binoculars as Thelma drives off.

"I feel for you, girlfriend," she says, recalling her fall out with Frank. "Trainers can be such pricks."

Tara reasoned had she seen Thelma Carson earlier, she may not have had to open Pandora's Box.

"Well, it's too late now. The genie is out of the bottle. I know it…I feel it. There is no telling what was going on inside that head of his when I left his office, but I'm sure he wasn't showering me with flowers and chocolate," she says with certainty.

The thought on Tara's mind now is Daniel's next move. The shift in energy she felt in his office was very strong and like nothing she had ever felt. Tara is convinced she has set ominous machinery in motion that Daniel may not be able to stop. In the process, Tara is more convinced that she has put someone's life in danger, possibly her own daughter's. She suspects Daniel will be reluctant to act on the compulsion to perform his grim fantasy for fear that he may be under surveillance. However, Tara feels it is just a matter of time before the urge will be too strong for him to overcome.

The overwhelming question on her mind is; *Will I be able to stop it?*

Tara grabs her phone as it rings. She reads the display screen and instantly recognizes the number.

"Agent Jenkins," she answers, somewhat relieved to get a break.

"Sorry to get back to you so late," the Agent says apologetically. "I do have some information on the proxy case you were referring about."

"Great," Tara responds.

"The case was in 1976 in LA. It didn't directly involve Chief Nirez, who was a junior detective at the time, but a close associate of his, a Detective Bo Santos. He'd been a detective for only seven years but had a boatload of commendations and was considered one of the best detectives in the department. The chief made a statement referring to Santos being his mentor, so they were probably very close. The killer's name was Randy Cox. He was a state worker at the California Department of Licensing. Mr. Cox claimed five victims with Detective Santos being the fifth. According to case records, the detective got a lead from his sister, Maria, who also worked at the Department of Licensing. On two occasions, she observed Mr. Cox acting strangely after serving a customer. Two to three days later, there would be a murder reported on the news and she saw the victims looked strikingly similar to Randy's customers. Thinking it was more than a coincidence, she got in contact with her brother. Somehow, Detective Santos became convinced Randy Cox was indeed his killer and his victims were proxies for his customers. He pursued Mr. Cox for months then suddenly the detective went silent. Many thought he had gone deep cover but unfortunately, someone discovered his body in a scrap metal yard. Detective Tanner…you still there?" the Agent asks, noticing her phone was deathly silent.

"I'm still here," Tara acknowledged, seeing some likeness in her case.

"What about the killer? Do you have anything else on him?"

"Yes, I do, and here is where it gets interesting. Six months after Detective Santos's death, an apparent suicide was reported that turned out to be Randy Cox. He left a suicide note confessing to the five killings."

"So what's interesting about that?"

"Well, I did a background check on him; he was Marine Force Recon and had done three tours in Nam."

"Well, that's interesting," Tara says, seeing the special forces connection between Randy Cox and Daniel Wade.

"With that kind of background, Mr. Cox was more than capable of taking out a top notch cop like Santos," the agent adds. Tara clearly recognizes the sense of urgency in the agent's voice. "Detective, you're one of the best at what you do, but you really need to be careful with Mr. Wade."

CHAPTER 19

Predator Or Prey

Hours have passed since Tara's departure and the most intense, violent and graphic attack of hallucinations Daniel has ever experienced. Since then, he has spent most of that time mercilessly punishing the heavy bag on the training floor as a quick fix to satisfy his true urge. Exhausted, and in a much calmer state, he sits on a bench while sweat drips off his muscular frame.

"You are a clever one, Detective, but not as clever as you think," Daniel says under his breath. He refuses to give her full credit. *Somehow, you stumbled on a stroke of luck and managed to connect a few dots*, he says to himself. He is positive that no physical evidence or eyewitnesses can link him to any of the killings.

Daniel suspects Tara was merely fishing on a hunch when they met in his office. He believes she did catch his skin flush for an instant, but feels that would not have been enough to convince her.

"I can't believe I let her get under my skin like that," he says, now angry with himself. "She tried to rattle my cage with her smart ass comment."

Even though Tara's efforts triggered his unprecedented attack, he refuses to acknowledge that it worked. Daniel is convinced that he is not just the detective's prime suspect but thinks she believes, beyond a doubt, that he is La Flore's killer. His verdict is based on events that happened after she left his office.

Tara walks out of the office when the attack she provoked hits him like a wrecking ball leaving him in a cold sweat. Later, Thelma walks into his office to find him perched on his desk.

"Daniel, are you ok?" she asks.

"Yes, Thelma, I'm fine."

She approaches him, dries his face with her towel and then gently caresses it.

"There," she says affectionately. "I just had the strangest thing happen with the woman who just left."

"Oh yeah, what was it?" Daniel asks with keen curiosity.

"Well, when she saw me, her skin went completely white and she had the most bizarre look on her face...like she'd seen a ghost."

Seeing Daniel's anxiety, Thelma is wary but undeterred from revealing the reason for her visit.

"You know, Bob is out of town for a few days and it's been a while since we've, you know...spent time together. Maybe a good roll in the hay is just what the doctor ordered," she said, caressing his arm. She dotingly placed her forearms across his shoulders as her hands stroked the back of his neck. "It can relieve your stress and anxiety. Don't worry," she moves closer whispering softly in his ear, "You can be as rough as you like."

Daniel looks Thelma squarely in the face. His look tells her he is not up for her offer. Getting the message, Thelma slowly releases him.

"What about tomorrow night?" she asks, knowing the answer will not be good. Daniel turns away for a moment, and then gives Thelma the same disinterested look.

"Ok...I see," she says, thoroughly disappointed. "Goodbye, Daniel. We're training tomorrow, aren't we?"

"Of course," he replies, his mind clearly somewhere else.

"Good. Do take care," Thelma says with a half-hearted smile before strolling off.

***

After recalling this episode, Daniel hones his thoughts on Tara. He continues to sit on the bench, now completely recovered from his long and physically exhausting ordeal.

"You think you've got it all figured out now don't you, Detective?" he asks aloud in a low tone, thinking about her next move.

"If that's the case, then you must also be afraid, afraid you've jeopardized someone, afraid that person is going to die for you. Oh, the possibilities," Daniel says, sprawling to stretch his limbs. "Whose blood is going to be on your hands, a complete stranger's, someone close to you, a sister, a daughter perhaps?"

Daniel pauses for a moment and looks across the training floor and into the early night sky displayed in his office window.

I know you're out there watching me. You think my compulsion is too strong for me to contain and it won't be long before I have to act on it. All you have to do is to wait for my blunder and foil the crime. Is that the plan? In that case, you really underestimate me, Daniel thinks, knowing his last comment was merely a bluff. The unprecedented nature of this last attack conjured his urge to a level he has never felt.

I welcome your challenge, Detective, but I'm afraid you can't stop me. No one can.

Hours later, Daniel's nude body twitches periodically under a thin bed sheet during the early a.m. His closed eyelids do little to hide the rapid eye movement signaling a dream that seems all too real.

His face and body are in full tiger stripe camouflage while he runs with amazing speed and stealth through the moonlit night and thick woods. His hazel eyes appear to glow against the olive green and black stripes on his face. He a sees a small number of dark figures in the moonlight scattered about, on patrol.

"You have your orders," a heavy voice says in his head, *"Kill the enemy."*

Daniel's eyes become narrow assessing each target. With flawless and lethal precision, a mangled pile of lifeless human remains is all that is left of the small patrol. Looking down upon the grisly sight, Daniel sees the bodies of Terri Gibson, Kelly Vogel, Barbara Jones, Cedric Wells and Penny

Keester. He looks around when a woman's voice in the distance startles him.

"Danny...Danny," the voice calls out.

Instantly, he finds himself on the training floor at his studio. The dark instrument of death that he was seconds earlier is now void of camouflage and wears his daily training garb. His face brightens when the striking blonde calling him emerges from the cardio room.

"Elaina," he says, overjoyed to see her.

"Where were you?" the woman asks.

"Oh, I was taking care of some pressing matters."

The two greet each other with an embrace that makes every part of him feel alive.

"So, Danny, what are we training today?"

"Well, today is Wednesday, so it's legs for you, my dear."

"Ugh, do we have to? I'm just not in the mood for it," Elaina laments.

"Ok...ok," he says with a pleasant demeanor. "What are you in the mood for?" He asks, smiling as he walks over to set up the abdominal machine for their ritual warm up.

"Justice," the heavy voice with a southern hint replies.

Daniel staggers and his pleasant smile dissipates at the sound of the strangely familiar accent that is clearly not his client's. He quickly turns to see Tara where Elaina was standing, holding a blonde wig in one hand and a menacing

Glock in the other. The room suddenly goes dark and quickly fills with a shadowy mass of several backup officers standing behind Tara, aiming their laser sights on him. She stands motionless.

"You lose, Daniel," her voice rings with a calm conviction.

Given no time to react, the lasers disappear from the bright muzzle flashes piercing the darkness from behind her.

The thunderous explosion from the volley of gunfire hurls him out of his sleep. Daniel sits up in his bed, now wide-awake with beads of sweat glistening on his skin and his heart racing. After a while, he falls back on his pillow, gazing at the ceiling. Bits of his dream flash in his head before his mind asks, "Well, Detective, who's the predator and who's the prey?

CHAPTER 20

Thanatos

The voices tell me to kill. When they do, one of you will die. Citizens of La Flore, for months you have gotten to know me, to fear me. Do not fear me. Fear the voices. Like my brothers and sisters, I am just a soldier, an instrument. You may know some of them, Ted Bundy, Mary Ann Cotton, Randy Woodfield, David Berkowitz...the list goes on, forever. We all serve the same master, the same voices. Your police department cannot protect you as they could not protect my victims or your fellow citizens. Like your incompetent mayor and police chief, LFPD is pathetic. They will never catch me. They deceived you by detaining a homeless bum as a suspect, all the while having full knowledge he did not do any of my work. They treat you like children, too afraid to hear the truth. I will tell you the truth. I bashed Terri Gibson's head in with a sledgehammer. The voices wanted to know what she was thinking. Her brains splattered on my face; the taste was sweet. I suffocated Kelly Vogel and desecrated her body because the voices wanted to have some fun. I disemboweled Barbara Jones with a butcher knife. The voices told me she was host to an alien life form and I had to deliver it. The delivery was a success and you should be relieved to know the alien life form is now happy and healthy. I decapitated Cedric Wells with a cleaver. The voices hate homosexuals and they wanted me to kill their leader. Penny Keester was poisoning the minds of your children with the filth in her books. The voices wanted me to do something special for the children. You should be thankful. This will be the only letter you receive. The next time you hear from me, you will know. One of you will die.

Thanatos

LFPD, KAPO 7 News and The La Flore Herald newspaper received the handwritten letters in red ink inside manila envelopes. La Florians anxiously devoured its contents once the letter found its way to the Internet. Tara is incredulous about news of the letter as she drives in late to the precinct after a long and exhausting night. Her surveillance of Daniel ended at one-thirty a.m. Tara trailed Daniel to his modest yet immaculate adobe rambler, making sure he knew there were eyes on him. She circled his block several times before parking near his home in plain sight. Tara's plan is to remain conspicuous over the next few days. Then, she will go covert, turning her surveillance into a shell game. Daniel knows she cannot watch him 24/7. What he soon will not know is when Tara is watching him and when she is not.

In late morning, Tara arrives at Division to find the office abandoned. Instinctively, she goes to the conference room where she walks into a standing room only meeting in progress. She scans the scene. A knot in her stomach forms at what she sees. There is audience comprised of detectives and uniformed officers. She spots Detective McVey, who is unable to see her. Tara sees Detective Cummins and they make eye contact. His expression reminds her of a pouting child whose sand box has unwanted guests and his agitation has him feeling more than ready to shoot someone. She sees Commander Johnson and Chief Nirez standing at the front of the conference room. Chief Nirez appears engaged with the speaker, but Commander Johnson, with arms crossed, appears aloof.

As Tara and the commander make eye contact she hears, "Detective," a commanding voice projects. The speaker looks down at his list to make sure he gets the name correct, "Tanner," he says confidently. "Glad to see you can finally join us," he says with a hint of sarcasm.

"She was on surveillance last night," Commander Johnson says.

"Surveillance of what?" the speaker asks.

"Surveillance of another suspect," Johnson answers, reaching the end of his rope.

"Well…not anymore," the speaker says confidently.

Tara, though not in the best of moods, is impressed.

Of all of the assholes I've met in my life, this one manages to sky rocket to the very top of my shit list within a matter of seconds. *Is he really that gifted or did that require special training?*" she asks herself.

Tara's attention hones in on the tall John Malkovich look-alike with a bad comb over, and more than likely, Detective Cummins's target. She immediately recognizes the badge dangling around his neck. "He's a Fed, a profiler no doubt…Great," Tara groans under her breath. She studies the task force of two men and one woman accompanying him, all wearing the same badge. To Tara, and many others in the audience, the agents appear much younger and seem less experienced than the ostentatious speaker; making them look less like a task force and more like an entourage.

"Detective Tanner, let me pause and introduce myself. I'm Special Agent Raymond Mack and I'm with…"

"I know who you're with, Special Agent," Tara interrupts. "That's why you're special."

Her remark has an effect on the audience. Some think Tara is being blatantly disrespectful. Others think the same, but feel Agent Mack rightfully deserves it. From the corner of her eye, she sees Detective Cummins gesture her a fist bump.

Chief Nirez leans towards Commander Johnson, "That was totally uncalled for," he sternly whispers to Johnson.

The commander is motionless, though the expression on his face clearly says, "Oh, no it wasn't."

Members of the task force exchange darting glances, expressing disbelief that someone is standing up to their boss.

"No need to get testy, Detective. We're on your side," the agent says, wearing a crocodile smile.

"Really now," Tara says to herself.

"DC tasked us at the behest of your governor and mayor to help out since you seem to be having some trouble getting the job done, Detective," the agent says, taking a swipe at Tara while continuing to smile.

"Now, continuing the profile before we were interrupted, the killer definitely has a beef with La Flore and in light of his stunt with the letters, he wants everyone in La Flore to know it. Therefore, we could be dealing with a city worker who is disgruntled because of a layoff. He might also be part of the corporate establishment that had a contract with the city that either has run its course, or had his funding cut. Either way, he believes the city is directly responsible for his woes and he is exacting his revenge. The voices do nothing but further validate his reason to kill. The killer is most likely a white male in his late thirties to late forties. There is a good chance he is married. This would amplify his resentment as he now sees his family having to suffer; or that he has to rely on his wife now being the breadwinner. Anyone familiar with Greek mythology knows that Thanatos is a word meaning "death". I believe the killer is using the name to instill fear. It is important that we act quickly. A life depends on it, if it hasn't been lost already. Also, just as luck went bad for him by losing his job, it can become good again. Meaning, he may land another job. In that case, he loses his resentment and subsequently his beef with La Flore. There is no longer a reason to kill and he simply…vanishes."

Despite his grating arrogance, the agent's compelling case and poignant delivery has Tara a bit awed.

This guy could sell snow to an Eskimo in the middle of a blizzard, she thinks, not realizing the amusement she found from her thought is clearly visible on her face.

"Is there something funny about what I just said, Detective?" the agent asks, now overtly agitated.

"No, no, Special Agent, you're doing fine," Tara responds, chuckling to herself.

She looks over at the commander and the chief. The chief looks furious and though Commander Johnson has had more than his fill of the agent, he now appears unhappy with her behavior over the past few minutes. There is a moment of silence and a bizarre calmness about the agent.

"Detective...could you come forward please?" he asks nonchalantly.

Not wanting to cause more trouble than she already has, Tara begrudgingly walks towards the agent.

"Stop...right there," he says, pointing to where she is standing.

Tara finds herself in the middle of the conference room. Her air of confidence masking her exposed feeling.

The agent stands straight and motionless with hands crossed behind his back displaying his trademark smile.

The scene takes on the look of a schoolgirl in the presence of a domineering schoolmaster. Tara watches the smile corrode from the Grinch looking figure standing in front of her. Then, the gloves come off.

"Detective Tara Tanner," he says, relishing what was about to come.

"How could I have forgotten that name? You were the lead detective in the Sexton debacle two years ago weren't you?" he asks coldly, as if cross-examining a witness. Tara remains silent and steadfast in her charade, though a bit shell-shocked.

"We studied that case quite a bit at the Bureau you know," he says, casually addressing Tara and the rest of the assemblage. "Although you were absolved of any liability...which after personal review, I find arguable, the case still teaches our new recruits how to not conduct an investigation. I would commend you for providing that valuable information. But, with the case resulting in the tragic and needless deaths of a mother and her child, in addition to the nasty stain put on your then unblemished department, I feel such an accolade would be...inappropriate."

Tara makes a scan of a room gone completely silent with all eyes upon her. Commander Johnson appears stoic and Agent Cummins is curious as to her next move. Tara knows her case cannot stand up to Agent Mack's since his case is based on someone who's actually admitted to La Flore's killings.

How in hell do I get myself into these messes? she asks herself. *Oh yeah...I'm Tara Tanner.*

With the suspense building, she diffuses the moment with what she sees as her only option.

"It was not my intention to find humor in, or belittle your case in any way, Agent Mack, and I sincerely apologize."

Tara has a déjà vu moment as the Sexton case, once again, rears its ugly head, conjuring its all-consuming cloud of negative energy. She can clearly see old wounds reopening among the group of officers and detectives.

It's like the past is coming back to haunt me, she thinks, the weight of days gone by bearing down upon her. *This time, I must make it right.*

CHAPTER 21

Daniel on the Low

It is not long after her spectacle with Agent Mack that Tara finds herself facing the music in Commander Johnson's office.

"You don't know how close you came to getting your ass suspended today, Detective!"

Tara stands in front of the heavy oak desk in the middle of a ten-minute royal ass chewing, which is brutally unpleasant...but justified, in her opinion.

"You're walking on very thin ice, Detective. Be careful how and where you step. Understand? I'm not going to bat for you again...I'm tired of it."

Tara knows a simple apology will not absolve her behavior or ease the commander's anger at this point.

Hesitantly, she is compelled to present the burning question in her head.

"What about Daniel Wade?" she asks in a solemn but urgent voice.

The commander sits back in his plush leather chair and contemplates. Tara, realizing she is light years from his good side, tactfully weighs in.

"I know Agent Mack's case is very plausible, and this Thanatos character has confessed to being the killer. But based on Agent Mack's proposed profile, I can't buy a city worker having the ability to kill without leaving a trace until we know more about him. I had Agent Jenkins look into the Chief's case. Yes, the killer, Randy Cox, was a city worker, but he was also Marine

Force Recon and served three tours in Nam, making him more than capable of this type of killing and taking out a top cop like Detective Santos. We know Daniel Wade's background gives him many of the same capabilities as Randy Cox. Until we find out more about Thanatos, I...I feel someone needs to stay on him."

Silence fills the office. Tara sits calmly, though her heart races waiting for the commander's response.

"Agreed," Johnson reluctantly concludes. He remains silent for a moment, then says, "Because of the shit storm generated by those letters, the blowback we got for detaining Harry, the media madness that's gone viral, and the entire city going cuckoo for Thanatos; our main mission is to apprehend or if need be, kill our new primary suspect. That's the direction the brunt of our resources, along with Agent Mack and his team of sycophants are heading."

The commander is silent once more, thoughtfully considering whether he is making the right decision, and then looks Tara squarely in the face. "I want you to stay on Mr. Wade. Keep it on the low...I mean it! If you even so much as fart on this case, I won't hesitate to pull the plug on Daniel Wade and you, is that clear?"

"Crystal," Tara responds.

"Besides, it will keep you away from your obnoxious boyfriend, Agent Mack, and spare Division another lover's spat. Good day, Detective."

Johnson's massive hands snatch a pile of paperwork off his desk and sift through them as Tara remained, standing at his desk.

"Commander, I want to apol…"

"I said good day, Detective!" he says, continuing to sort through the paperwork.

She walks out of his office, thinking how much she must be on his bad side. The ass chewing and putting her on a tight leash was bad enough, but she shudders to think that he would conjure such a dreadful thought. *Me and Agent Mack…lovers?* She cringes. *Only after a twelve pack and a Valium.*

Despite her ordeal with the commander, Tara is overwhelmed with relief at his decision. Realizing there is no margin for error, she is convinced that if the commander had her pursue Thanatos instead of Daniel, someone would be her proxy, facing certain death. She focuses on how Daniel may take the sudden turn of events. Tara suspects Daniel does not feel wronged that someone else is taking credit for his killings.

If anything, he's probably relieved. As much as he may see this twist of fate as a window of opportunity, I feel he will still be cautious in spite of his mounting urge to play out his grim fantasy. He underestimated me once. He won't underestimate me again.

On La Flore's west side, "There are really, really evil, sick and twisted people in this world. Can you believe this Thanatos guy? Did you read his letter? He bashes a person's brains in, suffocates someone, cuts a person's stomach open over some twisted idea that he is delivering some alien life form, decapitates someone, and horribly mutilates a person and then brags he will never be caught. Tell me how such evil fucks like Thanatos or whatever his real name is, come to exist?" Becky fumes, livid, frustrated and a bit frightened.

"Does it really matter?" Daniel asks calmly, perched on his desk. "Evil can come from the most unlikely of places. All that matters now is catching this guy and bringing him to justice."

"Bring him to justice? Becky shouts, as if she has better plans for Thanatos.

"You know, Dan, you're my boss and you're like a big brother, but you can be so righteous at times it's nauseating."

"I didn't specify the manner of justice," he replies. "That, my dear, I will leave up to whatever's in that sadistic little head of yours."

"Thank you, since you don't have the stomach for my kind of justice."

"Oh, you'd be surprised," he says in a lighthearted tone.

"You think LFPD will catch him? she asks. "Thanatos punked them pretty bad in his letter. I'd really be pissed if I were a La Flore cop right now. If I were in charge, I'd have every cop and detective after this sick bastard. What do you think?"

"I don't know about every cop, but I'd sure have a lot of them looking for him," Daniel says, finding himself sizing up the playing field. *All except for…one*, his instincts caution him.

"Well, everything is closed up. Mr. Maddox had to reschedule for next week and Elaina called and confirmed for tomorrow morning. Is there anything you have for me before I go?"

"No, enjoy the rest of your day, and Becky?"

"What?"

"You really need to lighten up. I won't let Thanatos hurt you," he says earnestly, sensing her fear.

"Thanks," she responds graciously. "It's good to know there are guys like you in the world."

Becky strolls towards the door before stopping to turn and face her boss.

"Hey, got any big plans for tonight?" she cheerfully asks.

A cunning grin take hold of his face as he responds, "Maybe."

CHAPTER 22

A New Trainer

T *ara walks down the long corridor to the examination*
room. She passes Agent Sumner's office and sees him
sitting at his desk thumbing through papers. He looks at her
with an expression of condolence on his face. She passes
another office to see Kelly Vogel's husband sitting in a chair
staring at the floor, tears streaming down his face. He looks
at her with sorrow and loneliness. Tara reaches the entrance
to the examination room and sees a body lying on the exam
table completely covered by a surgical sheet. She walks over to
the table, her heart beating faster with every step. Staring at
the sheet, Tara's breath becomes heavy and uneven. She pulls
back the sheet to shoulder level and is hit with a level of
heartache unfelt since the passing of her father. Sara lies
pristine but clearly dead. Tara wants to flee as she can't bear
to look at her daughter any longer, but is completely
paralyzed.

Sara's eyes slowly open wide, displaying cloudy lifeless
pupils, filling with tears. Her head turns slowly to face her
mother, frantically fighting her paralysis. Looking into
Tara's eyes, the expression on her daughter's face asks,
"Why did he do this to me, why me instead of you?"

***

Tara snaps out of her sleep. She takes a moment to
clear her mind as her head is nestled against the car
door. She checks her watch to see how long she has
been out. Sitting up, Tara stretches as best she can
within the confines of her front seat.

"Man, this is really starting to get old," Tara says, grabbing her binoculars and peering into Daniel's training studio.

Months have passed since her first stakeout on Daniel. Tara feels the shell game has worked so far, despite huge lapses of time within her surveillance operation. There have been no killings. This reassures her since none of Daniel's victims were discovered longer than seventy-two hours after they'd been killed. Tara knows that time is Daniel's ally and will eventually shift the balance in his favor.

"How soon will he realize that it already has?" she asks herself.

Over the next few months, life goes on in La Flore. No surprise to Tara, Thanatos has not claimed a single victim, though there have been numerous supposed sightings of him by hysterical La Florians and attention seekers yearning for their five minutes of fame. Meanwhile, LFPD's task force on Thanatos is reduced to a small but hardnosed skeleton crew. Agent Mack concludes the killer has landed a job and has blended back into society…for now.

La Flore's mayoral race is in full swing with heavy campaign blows thrown from the onset. Mayor Hondo Saks and the Republicans accuse candidate Eddie Lamar and the Democrats of fabricating Thanatos, claiming the personal attacks in his letter were designed by Lamar's propagandists to make him and the chief appear incompetent. Likewise, Eddie Lamar and the Democrats accuse Mayor Saks and the Republicans of fabricating Thanatos and setting up the task force as a tool of fear, and a dog and pony show to appear competent, all while the real killer is still at large. In light of the accusations from each party, Tara is certain Daniel is voting Republican.

Meanwhile, in a difficult and heartbreaking decision, Tara chooses to find another trainer. Frank's motivating training sessions and encouragement helped her overcome a very difficult period in her life for which she will always be grateful. However, Tara knows it is the deeper, more personal reasons she chose Frank that brought her to this verdict; reasons that made her vow never to become like her mother. Sasha Ladd was recommended to Tara by Agent Jenkins. A national level masters figure competitor and former Olympic level sprinter, the forty year old is a no-nonsense trainer of the highest caliber. Her studio, Life Long Fitness, is a hub for the residents of La Flore's north side. Tara enjoys Sasha's high-energy training and her sisterly companionship, but she knows in her heart she will deeply miss her intense and at times intimate sessions with Frank.

It is early evening and Tara and Megan are watching a heated episode of Survivor. For the first time in weeks, she is managing to relax, put her feet up and enjoy some quality time with her daughter. The two snack on a large bowl of light popcorn. Megan sips on lightly sweetened lemonade and Tara enjoys a Riesling in a short heavy glass.

"Can I have a sip?" Megan asks, looking up at her mother with a beaming smile.

She gets an affectionate but unequivocal "no way" look from her mother. Tara is halfway through her second glass as Megan is not the only person she has sights on for quality time this evening.

"Freeze the TiVo while I fill up," Tara says heading towards the kitchen.

"Mom...you're going to be an alcoholic."

"Meg...no I'm not, and who's the parent here?"

Megan stares at the motionless screen when suddenly, the phone rings.

"I'll get it," Tara yells from the kitchen.

Moments later, the piercing shatter of the heavy glass crashing onto the kitchen floor startles Megan. Concerned, she yells,

"Mom, Mom, Are you alright?"

CHAPTER 23

Where's Sara?

Tara quickly tries to regain her composure after the phone call as she hears Megan approach the kitchen.

"Mom, is everything alright?" Megan asks worried about her mother.

"Yes, Meg, I'm fine," Tara replies as she begins cleaning up the wine and pieces of shattered glass on the floor. "I just knocked over my glass that's all," she says in an effort to keep it together. "Tell you what, why don't you go watch the rest of Survivor. Mommy's got some business to take care of."

"Ok," Megan says and leaves the kitchen unconvinced.

Upon finishing, Tara sits at the kitchen bar and closes her eyes massaging both temples with the tips of her fingers. Her mind cannot help but replay the event from moments earlier.

"This is Tara speaking."

"Mrs. Tanner, this is Mary, Sara's roommate."

"Oh. Hi Mary. What's up?"

"I was just wondering if Sara was staying with you. She hasn't been here or answered her cell phone for a couple of days."

Tara's eyes open as the piercing sound of shattering glass replays in her head. Knowing Sara, Tara realizes there could be a number of reasons why she has gone off the radar. This is nothing she has not done before. In light of Daniel Wade's mounting urge to kill and his selection of proxy victims, Tara cannot help but be gravely concerned that her daughter would be his next proxy.

Tara finds herself in a precarious predicament. Her first inclination is simply out of the question as the scenario rages in her head.

Daniel is in the middle of an intense training session with a gorgeous supermodel as Chris Isaak's "Baby Did a Bad, Bad Thing" blares from the speakers. Tara marches purposefully into the studio with her Glock in hand, unlocked and loaded. She casually nods at Becky while walking past the front desk and onto the training floor. Daniel's back faces her as he motivates the model in a grueling set of crunches. Suddenly he hears a familiar voice with a hint of southern seduction,

"Daniel, I have something special for you."

Curious, Daniel turns around to see Tara standing a few feet away wearing a face with lethal intentions. He sees the menacing firearm in her hand. A smile changes Daniel's face as she once again feels the eerie shift in energy.

"Well, if it isn't the complete bitch I told Becky about. You brought that for me? Really, you shouldn't have." The two stare at each other for a moment while the music blazes with prophetic lyrics.

"Well don't just stand there. Show me and the nice lady why you're here."

"Gladly."

Without hesitation, Tara swiftly takes aim with her Glock and unloads all of its deadly cargo into Daniel's head and torso piercing flesh, organs and shattering bone. As she turns to leave, she sees Becky frozen in place and astonished at the sight of the model, now hysterical as Daniel lies on top of her spilling his contents. She approaches Becky.

"Your boss is a jerk you know. Do you have a daughter?"

Becky vigorously shakes her head no.

"Well Becky, it's a mom-daughter thing. You wouldn't understand."

As Tara walks away, she turns back to Becky.

"Tell Barbie, soaking her outfit in ammonia will get that out."

Upon scanning the scene once more to see the model's powder blue outfit is now completely drenched in blood, body fluids and brain matter, she adds,

"Hmm, maybe not."

Tara weighs all of her options. As much as she would love to administer some personal justice, she begrudgingly realizes that she has to play the waiting game.

"Daniel's victims are discovered no longer than seventy-two hours after they were killed. Sara's been missing forty-eight hours; that leaves twenty-four hours. Within twenty-five hours, I will find out whether this is just a strange coincidence or my daughter has become one of Daniel's victims," Tara thinks out loud.

She knows in order to prevent being pulled from the case; her concerns about Sara must be kept under wraps, even from her family. Most importantly, Tara has to hold it together for the next twenty-four hours as if she had never gotten the news of her missing daughter, even though it dominates her every thought, causing ever-mounting anxiety.

The next morning brings a gray and dismal overcast sky that matches Tara's mood.

"Thank you for last night," Dale says giving Tara an affectionate kiss before heading off to work.

"No, thank you," She says forcing a large smile while caressing his face.

Tara feels relief knowing she pulled off convincing her husband that she was into their night together as much as he was. Dale suddenly finds himself in a firm embrace in which he lovingly reciprocates. He gently kisses her forehead as they continue their embrace.

"Are you ok?"

"I am now...Just hold me for a minute." She takes the time to lose herself.

"A rough day in front of you, sweetheart?"

There is a brief pause as she thinks over all of the potential scenarios the day could bring, "Possibly."

As Dale heads off to work, he leaves her standing in front of their living room window peering up at clouds that seem to be getting darker and gloomier with the passing of time. She crosses her arms to fend off the chill that has taken hold of her.

"Sara, baby where are you?" Tara asks desperately trying to avoid seeing the foreboding clouds looming overhead as harbingers of worse things to come. Feeling completely helpless, Tara grudgingly must continue to play out the dismal and stressful waiting game.

CHAPTER 24

Tara's Meltdown

The thick dark clouds continue to repel all manner of sunlight making the day appear as night. Hours have passed as Tara finds herself obsessed with time. While driving to the precinct, she was compelled to drive by Daniel's studio for a stint of surveillance, but refrained in fear that she might lose it and impose the personal justice she had fantasized. In that instant, Tara saw a glimpse of Daniel's twisted and distorted world.

At her desk, anxiety continues to build as she sifts through mounds of paperwork and photos. She is interrupted by Detective Cummins, who has been observing her from his desk.

"Hey Tanner, how's everything going on this beautiful day?" he asks. Seeing that his sarcastic humor had no effect on her, he asks in a more concerned tone, "No, really, how are you doing?"

Tara makes shallow nods with her head as she dwells on Cummins's question. "I'm at peace," Tara responds in a calm voice. "I'm at peace with whatever today may bring."

"What the hell is that supposed to mean?" Cummins asks, wearing a puzzled look on his face.

"It just means this case has taken such a toll on me that I can now roll with any punch it throws at me."

"Now that's impressive. You'll get through anything with that attitude," he says. "So, how's Dale doing?"

"Dale is doing well. The company just landed a big security contract, so he's busy," she responds.

"How's my little girl Meg?"

"Meg is eleven going on twenty-five," Tara says with a chuckle.

"Mark my words Tanner, Meg is going to be the first female President or else there's going to be hell to pay."

The two burst out in a brief fit of laughter.

"I hear Sara is thinking about being a journalist. That's great! You should be proud of her," Cummins says, completely oblivious that beneath the thin surface of confidence and assurance his colleague displays, she is an emotional train wreck.

"Yes, Cummins, I'm very proud of her. I think she's finally starting to turn her life around."

"Amen to that sister," Cummins says. "I get the feeling she will have a good life thanks to you."

At that moment, all Tara wants to do is cry and vent how she has nine more agonizing hours before she knows whether her daughter is alive or dead, and how it may all be her fault. "You're a good friend, Cummins," Tara says.

"I'll take that compliment from you any day."

The two are drawn to the commotion of Commander Johnson, Chief Nirez and Special Agent Mack making their way to the commander's office. As the three men walk by, Tara and Cummins find themselves in a stare down with Special Agent Mack. The men enter the commander's office closing the door behind them.

"We must be in for another briefing with the anointed one," Cummins says.

"I'd love to go back in time and take out the school bully who beat him up for his lunch money over the years. It sure as hell would make our lives a lot easier right now," he says earnestly.

"Amen to that," Tara responds.

A short time later, Tara finds herself in the middle of the briefing accurately forecast by Detective Cummins. In no mood for a fight with Agent Mack, this time, she resigns to keeping her mouth shut. Barely aware that Agent Mack is speaking, his words are moot as she tallies the time, knowing there are still five hours remaining until she learns the fate of her daughter. She notices an officer approach Commander Johnson, who is standing in front of the conference room, and hand him a slip of paper. Upon reading the paper, Johnson looks directly at Tara. Her emotions go on high as she desperately refrains from showing them. Tara knows a meltdown here and now will not only get her pulled from Daniel's case, but also could mean the end of her career as a detective.

The Commander interrupts Agent Mack by approaching him and whispering in his ear. He hands

Agent Mack the slip of paper and returns to where he was standing. As Agent Mack examines the paper, Tara's emotions are in overdrive, and despite the watchful eye of Commander Johnson, she finds her imminent category five meltdown increasingly harder to mask. Upon examining the paper, Agent Mack briefly stares at the large assembly of detectives and uniformed officers.

"It appears our killer has struck again. The body of a dark haired woman presumed to be in her twenties has been found in the town of Enid."

Tara secretly clenches her fist, displaying white knuckles in a desperate and final attempt to fend off her meltdown.

"Even though the victim was found two hours from La Flore, the MO of the killing and some incriminating evidence prompted local law enforcement to contact us," Agent Mack says.

"Did they identify the victim?" a detective asks.

"No," Agent Mack responds. "According to this report, they just found the body a couple of hours ago. This poor girl was beaten beyond recognition."

Tara's heart feels like a lead weight in her chest. "I've killed my baby," she tells herself as her eyes began to well with tears. *I'm sorry Sara. I'm so sorry.* Tara's meltdown is nearly full blown as she stands up and makes a desperate attempt to walk casually from the conference room before it gets out of control. Her exit draws the attention of Commander Johnson, who has been eyeing her with some concern the entire time.

Tara staggers slightly to the women's restroom on legs weakened by the latest news. Seeing that the room is empty, she walks over to the row of sinks and looks into the mirror. She sees her reflection as tears began to stream down her face. Tara is moments from collapsing into sobs when her cell phone rings. She retrieves it to see Sara's name displayed. Though it is a welcome sight, she is unsure who will answer: her daughter, or Daniel. She stares at the phone as it beckons her to answer. She hesitantly presses the answer button, knowing this is her moment of truth.

"Hello," she answers in a teary voice.

"Mom, is that you?"

The relief hits Tara like a speeding semi upon hearing her daughter's voice.

"Mom, you ok? You sound like you've been crying," Sara says. "What's wrong?"

"Are you ok?" Tara asks vehemently.

"I'm fine, Mom. Why wouldn't I be?

"Where have you been?" Tara asks, barely able to speak.

"Nic and I had a big fight and I had to get away for a while. I was ahead in my lab work and with Nic being the consummate prick that he is when he's promoting a concert, I figured now was the best time."

"Actually, it was the absolute worst time," Tara says between sniffles.

"What do you mean by the worst time? What's going on? Are Meg and Dale ok?"

"Never mind, everyone's fine. I'm just happy you're ok." Tara says.

"Mom," her daughter asks.

"Yes, Sara."

"Am I going to be like this when I'm your age?"

"I hope to God not," Tara answers with a chuckle as she begins to sound like herself again. "Apparently my actions have stressed you out for whatever reason, and I'm sorry," Sara says.

"Here's how you're going to make this up to me," her mother responds, sounding more and more herself with an occasional sniffle. Sara braces herself for the worst.

"Come to dinner tonight and spend some time with me."

"That's it?"

"That's it," Tara says.

"Ok, I don't mean to sound flaky, but I only have enough gas to get there, and I…"

"Don't worry about the gas. I'll fill your tank for the week."

"No joke?! Ok, I'll be there," Sara responds.

"If you want, we can even talk about Nic," Tara adds.

"Oh, Nic is so done!"

"Isn't that what you said three breakups ago?"

"Hey, Mom whose side are you on?"

"Dinner…tonight…Be there. You won't regret it."

"You don't have to tell me twice!"

A distinct click signals the end of their phone conversation. Tara stands motionless for a moment.

"Yes, Yes!" she screams silently, clenching her fists.

The good fortune about her daughter does not spare her the inevitable as she backs into a stall, sits down and erupts into silent, emotional and joyful sobs. She is having dinner tonight with her daughter, who just minutes before, she had presumed without a doubt, was dead. At this moment, Tara Tanner is unquestionably, the happiest mother in the world.

CHAPTER 25

The Storm

That evening, Sara enjoyed her all-time favorite meal, her mom's rich homemade baked triple layer lasagna, buttery garlic bread and a green salad with an olive oil, vinegar and hint of lemon dressing. Tara called Dale in the middle of a busy project and gave him strict orders to be home for dinner, on time, or else. Needless to say he was ten minutes early. Dale had to return to work after what he considered, without a doubt, the best meal he'd had in a while. So good, he took the remains of the abundant feast to his famished and grateful partners. The night ended with Tara and her daughters on the sofa. Sara rested her head on Tara's shoulder while Megan's head was nestled in her lap. She fondly recalled an incident that happened shortly after Dale left. Sara received a call from her boyfriend Nic. An argument soon erupted followed by talks of making up, followed by another argument, then talk of marriage.

Megan rolled her eyes at the raging spectacle. She turned to Tara, "Mom?" she asked.

"Yes Megan."

"Am I going to be like this when I'm her age?"

"I hope to God not."

***

The pleasant memory of last night fades from Tara's mind as she is now halfway on her drive to Enid. The dark, heavy clouds of yesterday persist accompanied by periodic claps of thunder and brilliant streaks of lightning. The murky overcast blankets the flat rustic terrain as far as the eye can see. Tara is finally coming down from the euphoria caused by her daughter's good fortune when a grim reality sets in. The calm reflective expression on her face a mere minute before, gradually morphs into a visage that is sharply focused. Fortunately, her daughter was spared Daniel's wrath but unfortunately, Jessica Stoval, was not.

Tara finally arrives at the rural town. In no time, she finds the modest size brick building that serves as both City Hall and the police department. She walks into a spacious area and sees two doors. On the doors are mounted large handsome black placards trimmed in copper with bold white letters. Tara heads to the door where the placard reads "Police." The portly middle-aged desk sergeant watches her enter. Caught off guard, and being a long time since an attractive woman has approached his desk, he takes immediate and drastic action. He sweeps the package of Hostess Ding Dongs, bag of Cheetos and liter of Doctor Pepper from his desk. Hastily, he replaces them with a protein bar, bottled water and the latest edition of Flex Magazine.

The desk sergeant is oblivious that Tara has been watching the entire scene. She arrives at his desk and gives him a big smile. Thinking his quick maneuvering paid off, he is unaware that he overlooked the Cheetos crumbs and Ding Dong smears surrounding his mouth, prompting the real reason for Tara's smile.

"I'm Sergeant Wells. Can I help you, Miss?" he asks with a commanding voice.

"Sergeant Wells, I'm Detective Tanner from La Flore's Detective Division.

I'm here to examine the body of Jessica Stoval."

"Jessica Stoval?" a deep scruffy voice shouts from an office behind the Sergeant's desk. A silver haired man appears from behind the desk and approaches her. To Tara, the man in front of her clearly did not live up to the voice she had heard bellow moments earlier. His thin build, average height and heavily worn face faintly remind Tara of her father.

"So, Detective, what business would you have with the deceased since a team from La Flore was already here?" the man asks.

Looking at his badge, Tara knows she is addressing the head honcho, seeing the title "Chief" engraved on it. The chief catches a glimpse of the desk sergeant from the corner of his eye then turns his sights on him. After a quick assessment to validate his peripheral view, "Willie," the chief says with slight chagrin.

"Yes, Chief," the desk sergeant replies sharply.

"Go to the restroom and check yourself." The desk sergeant replies with a puzzled look on his face. "Trust me Willie, just go. You'll find out when you get there."

As the sergeant leaves the chief turns to Tara, "He's got his quirks about him but he's a good man," the chief says.

"I trust your judgment completely," Tara replies, attempting to gain brownie points.

"I'm Chief Moore," he says, holding out a hand to greet her and wearing a guarded face. Tara politely engages the handshake, surprised by the firmness of his grip. She can sense that he is cautious and quickly realizes she may have to break through some barriers in order to make any headway in seeing the body.

"As I mentioned, a team was here earlier lead by a Special Agent Mack. What is your association with this special agent, Detective?" the chief asks with a twinge of hostility.

"You don't want to know," she responds.

"Actually, I do."

Seeing the chief has obviously had a dose of Agent Mack's charm,

"Let's just say, Agent Mack and I don't sing each other praises. That's why I didn't come with the team."

There is a pause as the chief deliberates with lean forearms crossed.

"No, no, you're just being nice," he says. "Good move on coming up on your own, Detective. Pardon my French but I sure as hell couldn't have endured a forty minute car drive with him without blowing his fucking brains out."

"Couldn't have said it better myself, Chief," Tara mutters under her breath.

"In light of the evidence we presented, Agent Mack and his team weren't completely convinced Jessica Stoval's murder is the work of your Thanatos killer. What makes you think you'll see anything different?"

Not wanting to let on about Daniel, "Let's just say, I have a gut feeling," Tara replies.

"A gut feeling?" the chief responds with sarcasm.

"Yes, a gut feeling."

The two take a moment staring at each other. Subtle grins take hold of both their faces in unison as they realize they are birds of a feather.

The desk sergeant returns with a fresh face, a shave and wet hair combed back. He gets a look from the chief and Tara who are slightly amused by the overkill.

"Sergeant," the chief calls.

"Yes, Chief."

"Go and get one of the junior officers in the back to escort the good detective downstairs, and have them bring the evidence bag."

"Yes, Chief."

As the sergeant leaves,

"You know, Willie has been known to be quite the ladies man."

He gets a raised eyebrow from Tara.

"Just kidding," he responds with a grin. "I've got to roll up my sleeves and assist my officers in the field. The weather is about to get extremely nasty and you may have to consider being here awhile. If you do, we've got a spare room in the back where you can stay."

"Thank you," Tara says graciously.

Waiting for her escort, the room illuminates from a brilliant flash of lightening followed by a deafening burst of thunder. The thick, dark clouds finally release their load in a hammering downpour of rain as if waiting for this precise moment. She senses the weather getting worse with each passing moment, as time draws closer to seeing Jessica Stoval's body. The desk sergeant returns with an officer that clearly has GREEN written all over his face. In his early twenties, the officer looks much younger but is very enthusiastic and quite cute, scoring points with Tara.

"You know what to do Officer Novak, so be sharp," the sergeant says with authority.

"Yes, sir," the boyish looking officer replies.

"Yes, Sergeant, not yes sir. I work for a living, Officer Novak."

"Yes, sir…Sergeant."

After a pause, "Yeah," the sergeant responds showing some frustration. "He's all yours, Detective."

"This way please," the officer says, gesturing Tara to follow him.

He leads her down a narrow hallway towards the door that heads downstairs. She is particularly interested in the large plastic evidence bag the officer is carrying.

"May I be candid, Detective?" the officer asks.

"By all means, do," Tara responds.

"This weather is bizarre," the officer replies as the raging storm gains momentum. "I've never seen weather like this. It's almost as if something sinister is behind it. You know what I mean?"

"Interesting point," Tara responds, not wanting to admit that she really thinks he is spot on.

"I hear this is pretty bad. My class leader at the academy escorted the team earlier and passed out. It's kind of funny because he always called me a woos at the academy."

"I'm pretty sure you will fare much better than your former class leader," She says, giving the officer a shot of confidence.

Knowing who, how and what might have caused Jessica Stoval's deadly fate has Tara asking herself, "The question is...will I?"

CHAPTER 26

The Message

Tara and the officer arrive at a grey metal door with the title "Coroner" stenciled in large red letters. Upon entering, they walk to the doorway of a small office.

"Doc, you're still here," Officer Novak says, looking in. "The chief thought you'd left for the day."

Dr. Russell sits reclined in his office chair with feet crossed on his desk next to a half-empty glass and a fifth of Johnnie Walker. The storm continues to build, raging outside, but Dr. Russell, a distinguished yet practical looking man in his early sixties, looks as if he is poolside at a Vegas resort.

"Well, young man...I didn't," he replies with a broad beaming smile. "For some reason, I decided to stick around. Besides, I have a bottle here as well as at home. I see you brought a guest, and a pretty one at that."

Dr. Russell remains motionless but his eyes scan Tara from head to toe.

Tara politely interjects. "Hi, I'm Detective Tanner from La Flore's Detective Division," she says, engaging the doctor in a handshake.

She makes a quick assessment of her host. Despite his sparse surroundings and mellow demeanor, she sees he is by no means a lightweight in his field. Mounted on the wall behind him is a Pathology Degree from Emory University. She knows from talks with Agent Sumner that Emory has a long tradition of being the top pathology program in the nation. She also sees that he is a member of Emory's highly esteemed and very exclusive Forensic Pathology Fellowship.

What impresses her most is the photo of the doctor mounted on the most majestic looking thoroughbred she has ever seen.

"That's Romulus," he replies out of habit.

"So, do I call you Doctor or Mr. Russell?" Tara asks.

"Well, since we're in the middle of a storm from hell and I'm working on my second glass in the company of such a pretty lady, call me Steve.... Let me guess, coming from La Flore, you're here to see Jessica Stoval's body," Dr. Russell asserts.

"Yes, I am, with your permission," she responds respectfully.

"You don't need my permission, Detective. You wouldn't have gotten this far without first going through Otis."

"That's the chief," the officer leans over and tells her.

"By the way, that Mack fellow didn't come again by chance? He's one of the reason I'm having an extra one of these," the doctor says, gesturing at his glass.

"I'm happy to tell you that he did not come with me. I came alone."

He gulps the rest of his drink then ponders a moment.

"Yeah, I can easily see how spending forty minutes in a car with that guy would be absolute misery. I am sure without a doubt I would end up blowing his brains out. Well, let's get down to business, shall we?"

He dons his white lab coat giving him an entirely different persona. He looks Tara in the eye with a smile not quite as jovial as the one a moment earlier.

"What was done to Jessica Stoval is the other reason," he says, referring to why he was having an extra shot of Johnnie Walker. He looks over at the junior officer.

"This is pretty bad, even for my taste young man, and I've already had one of your comrades pass out on me. Are you in or are you out? The choice is yours."

"I'm in, Doc," Officer Novak responds, seeing this as the perfect opportunity to finally one up his former class leader.

Tara and Officer Novak follow Dr. Russell a short distance to the examination room. As they enter, she sees what appears to be a human body lying on the examination table, covered by a faded blue surgical sheet. What is about to happen hits Tara, causing her adrenaline to soar and her heart to race. She is about to meet her own death by what she strongly believes is the person who died in her place...her proxy.

"What was the cause of death?" she asks, struggling a bit to say the words.

"Acute blunt force trauma to an extent I'd never seen inflicted on a person. In other words...she was beaten to death," the doctor says. "This is stuff you typically see when a vehicle strikes a pedestrian at high speed. In this poor woman's case, the vehicle would have been a very large truck or a bus. She would have suffered much less being hit by the vehicle, that way she would have sustained all of her injuries at once. It took a while to do this and she suffered through most of it. The interesting thing is there were no blunt instruments or weapons used, just kicks, stomps and blows from other parts of the body. Whoever did this was up close and very personal. I can't imagine who could be angry enough to inflict this kind of damage on another human being, or that evil to this extent lives among us."

He pulls back the sheet exposing the battered, bloated and disfigured body of the victim, who was once the owner of a local day care. He gives Tara and the young officer a moment to recover from the initial sight of the grotesque display. The sight clearly affects Officer Novak. For an instant, his skin becomes pale and he feels faint, but recovers and now is enthralled by what he sees.

"What is the extent of her injuries?" Tara asks reluctantly, nearly paralyzed by an overwhelming need to know.

"I'll start from the bottom," the doctor replies. "The right lower leg is broken in three places and the left lower leg is completely shattered. The right knee is broken. Both thigh bones have multiple breaks. The pelvis is broken in two places. Five vertebrae are either broken or shattered. Five ribs are broken puncturing both lungs. Her sternum is shattered bruising her heart. Most of the abdominal organs, bruised. The left arm has multiple breaks. The right arm is interesting though, the only injury is a hyperextension breaking it at the elbow. All of the other injuries seem random but this injury was very precise and if she were alive at that point...very painful. The collar bone has multiple breaks and her throat is crushed."

Finally, the three finally gaze at the heart of the sight. Every bone in Jessica's head and face was shattered leaving it a formless, swollen mass.

"Need I continue?" He asks.

A deafening clap of thunder shakes the building and flickers the lights as the violent storm continues to build in intensity. Tara's expression tells the doctor that she has heard and seen quite enough.

"Can I see the evidence bag, please?" Tara asks the officer. Officer Novak hands her the clear plastic bag.

"Is there somewhere I can put the items?" she asks.

"Here," the doctor says, retrieving an instrument table. Tara empties the bag's contents onto the table.

"I'm going to need some gloves, Steve."

The doctor hands Tara a pair of surgical gloves. Her posture tells him, and the officer, that she is clearly in search of something, though she may not know exactly what. Tara suspiciously explores through the tattered and blood stained clothing, checking pockets. She checks the insides of bloodied shoes before turning her sights on a thick vinyl wallet.

Tara notices Officer Novak assessing the storm. She senses he feels there is a connection between her and this storm, which is unlike anything the three has ever experienced.

"This wallet was just found, correct?" She asks, holding it in her hand.

"Yes, that's how we identified the victim," the doctor responds. "We contacted the family and found out she had been missing for about two days."

Tara opens the wallet and lifts a leather flap revealing the victims driver's license. Tara and the officer hone in on the license's photo.

"A relative of yours?" he asks.

"No." She continues to look through the contents of the wallet.

"We've gone through the wallet content Detective. I don't think you'll find anything else of interest," the doctor says with uncertainty.

"I'd be inclined to agree with you if this were a man's wallet, Steve," Tara responds.

At that point, a peculiar sight catches her eye. A bulge inside the lining of one of the compartments prompts her to rub a finger delicately over it. "Hmm," she murmurs.

She tugs at the lining eventually separating it. Lodged snuggly inside the lining, she sees a folded piece of paper. "Steve, do you have something I can get this out with?" she asks.

"Sure thing," he responds. He hastily retrieves a pair of tweezers and hands them to her, appearing curious as to what she has found.

With surgical precision, she pulls on the paper, being particularly careful not to damage it. A barrage of thunder ensues, getting the trio's attention. She stares at the paper as it beckons her to open it. She meticulously unfolds the paper knowing this is her defining moment.

Is Jessica Stoval the victim of another killer or did she die in my place? Did Daniel win?

Upon opening it, she discovers a message.

"What is it?" Dr. Russell asks, seeing Tara's face go pale, then blank.

"What does it say?" Officer Novak asks, seeing the same reaction.

She gently places the paper on top of the pile of evidence on the instrument table. Dr. Russell and Officer Novak approach to see a simple message written in the victim's blood that reads,

"See what you made me do."

CHAPTER 27

The Drive Home

A clear and peaceful night accompanies Tara on the drive back to La Flore. The night is so peaceful, one would be hard pressed to believe there had just been a raging storm. A drive like this normally has Tara playing her favorite CD mix, listening to "Black Velvet" to connect with her southern roots, though she knows the song is by Canadians, but her mind is at odds between navigating the pitch black deserted highway and having flashbacks to what happened back in Enid.

Officer Novak looks at Tara, amazed but not surprised at how quickly the storm dissipates after she reads the note.

"Is there any special meaning behind that message, Detective?" Dr. Russell asks.

"No, not in particular," she answers.

"Uh huh," he counters.

"Well, gentlemen...it seems like the storm has abated, Tara says with a sigh of relief.

"Yeah...miraculous isn't it?" the doctor says with a touch of cynicism.

"As strange as this may sound, that's probably my cue to head back to La Flore. Officer Novak, you've been a great help and you have been especially helpful, Dr. Russell."

"Call me, Steve," the doctor says.

"Yes, of course...Steve. Well, thank you kindly. I will see myself out, I know the way."

After Tara leaves, the young officer and doctor remain frozen for a moment, stupefied over what just happened.

"I've never experienced anything like that, Doc. It was like something out of a Stephen King book."

"I'm pretty sure I have, but I was probably too drunk to remember it."

"Do you think she feels that Thanatos fella did this?"

"Let's just say, I've got a gut feeling that little lady and the special agent aren't looking for the same horse," the doctor says in a shrewd tone. "As a result of our uncanny experience; I think now would be a good time for me to consult with my friend Johnnie."

Unexpectedly, the officer responds, "Hell yeah."

The shimmering lights of La Flore are a welcome sight, illuminated in the distance like a vast galaxy in the blackness of space. Anger, guilt and frustration dominate Tara's emotions throughout the drive. She envisions Daniel Wade, amused as he writes his message with the blood of his victim. She can see his face splattered with blood, euphoric from the longing, violent and deadly release he had been abstaining from for months. Tara's mind delves deeper, making it more personal.

Not only did he get his prize, he beat me; though he had to go out of bounds to do it. So, that is how we are going to play this game, Mr. Wade? Bend the rules?

She hears Daniel's voice boastfully proclaim, fueling her anger,

I win Detective…You lose.

She sees Jessica Stoval's battered body lying on the examination table as Dr. Russell flips endless pages on a clipboard reading the long list of the victim's brutal injuries. Finally, out of sheer frustration, he tosses the clipboard over his shoulder.

"What the hell did you do to piss someone off like this?"

The doctor adds, fueling her guilt,

"Better Jessica Stoval than your daughter, isn't it, Detective?"

Tara knows that the reality is, despite her mind's clarity about Daniel Wade's guilt, her pursuit of him is presently an outside case at best. A case that has to be: "kept on the low" as Chief Johnson puts it. She is certain Agent Mack's power of persuasion will make Thanatos the center of interest. Tara is also aware Daniel Wade knows this and will surely use it to his full advantage. Feeling she has reached the end of her rope to get any backing from Commander Johnson, Tara proclaims to herself, venting frustration,

It's hard to catch a killer you can't identify. It's hell when you've identified a killer, but due to lack of evidence, you can't touch him.

Tara's cell phone illuminates, getting her attention. She checks her display, curious as to the number that she can't identify.

"Tara speaking," she says cautiously.

"Hello, Tara."

The voice on the other end needs no introduction. Instantly, the anger, guilt and frustration that accompanied her on the trip to La Flore fade and then vanish. Although her emotions begin to stir, the voice is, without a doubt, a pleasant surprise.

"Frank, It's good to hear from you."

"Have I caught you at a bad time?" he asks with some hesitation.

"No, no. I am on a drive back from Enid. It's just me and the road."

"I won't hold you up, but the reason I called is because I just picked up a new client. She is a former client of the trainer you are investigating. They recently had a big falling out."

Oh, like the one we had. Tara thinks.

She can sense Frank feels he may have put his foot in his mouth.

"I believe she has something that may be of interest to you."

"Great, what's her name?"

There is an awkward silence. "I was hoping to talk about it over lunch tomorrow, if that's ok with you."

Tara feels Frank has put her on the spot. Enticing as seeing him again sounds, she hesitates on her decision.

"It's ok if you say no. I will completely understand and won't bother you again."

"I would love to. You just caught me off guard, that's all."

"I'm sorry. That was not my intention."

"Don't be. I'd love to see you and catch up."

"How does Dimitriou sound?" he asks.

"Dimitriou is fine. I've never been there but I know where it is."

"Ok then, I will see you tomorrow. Is noon ok? I can adjust my schedule to whatever works for you," he says in a tone bordering on desperation.

"Make it two o'clock to avoid the lunch hour rush," she says.

"Very well. It will be good to see you again, Tara."

"I look forward to seeing you, Frank."

As they disconnect, Tara is keenly interested to know about Frank's new client and Daniel Wade. If what Frank says is true, then Daniel may be on the hunt for a proxy and she must act swiftly. She is equally interested to know how her emotions will hold up when she sees her old trainer again.

CHAPTER 28

Lunch at Dimitriou

The cloudless sunny sky is a welcome change for La Florians. Nestled in the city's midst is a quaint bistro known for its unique pasta wraps, salads and coffees. However, Dimitriou is best known as a popular after hours hang out for many of the live music and dance clubs nearby. Just before 2 p.m., Tara pulls into the sparsely occupied parking lot. Frank's black, immaculate Infiniti coupe immediately catches her eye and awakens her butterflies. A cheerful young host greets her as she enters.

"You must be Tara."

"Yes, I am."

"Please, follow me."

The host leads Tara to a secluded part of the establishment. Right away, she sees the back of Frank's broad shoulders peering over the top of the shallow booth.

Hearing the party draw near, Frank stands and faces them. For the first time in nearly a year, their eyes meet. Tara's eyes express gladness to see her old trainer while Frank's eyes are clearly overjoyed. His body language, in contrast is reserved, knowing he was the cause of their falling out.

"I've got it from here. Thank you," Tara tells the host.

"Hello, Frank," she says happily, as she approaches.

"Hey, Tara," he says with a glowing smile. The two reacquaint themselves with a warm but cautious embrace.

"You're looking fantastic," Frank says, sitting in the cherry wood booth.

"Thank you. I can see you're just as handsome as ever," she replies.

"So, what's good here?"

"Everything is great. The tab is on me, so eat up," he says cheerfully.

Tara, never one for eating heavily while on duty, orders a light crab salad with Dimitriou's signature herb dressing, on the side. Frank, though having a rapacious appetite and metabolism, suddenly feels the need to follow suit and orders a Tuscan steak salad with Dimitriou's authentic Greek dressing.

A sly grin takes hold of his face when the waiter brings out a basket of the house's special, warm, soft freshly baked bread with pieces of prosciutto, along with a small bowl of Dimitriou's butter, cambazola cheese and garlic spread. Intrigued at the sight and smell, Tara takes one of the bite-sized slices of bread and coats it with the pasty spread. She places the entire slice in her mouth. Frank watches in amusement as her face grimaces from the savory flavors. She quickly coats another slice, places it on her small appetizer dish and hurriedly shoves the basket over to Frank.

"Get that away from me," she says, causing Frank to chuckle. "That is so sinfully good I just might end up pregnant," she says in her mother's southern drawl. Laughter breaks the ice as they enjoy the lunch and each other's greatly missed company.

Later, Tara and Frank sit among empty plates. Their waiter approaches. "Can I get those for you?"

"Yes, please." Frank says.

"Is anybody ready for dessert?" the waiter asks.

Both decline and the waiter soon has the table cleared. Tara asks for more water and Frank requests another diet soda.

An awkward stillness grabs Frank, "So, I hear you've hired Sasha to be your trainer," he says.

"Yes, I did. She's great, Frank. She really is," Tara responds, hoping he will approve. He ponders for a moment, "I think it was a very good call on your part. I could see you two working very well together."

The stillness returns and Tara sees the cue to inquire about the young lover she found him with at his studio. She senses his apprehension as he braces for the moment. Despite her profound curiosity, she says, "The problem is I'm so bogged down with this Daniel Wade case that I can't get in to see her like I should."

"Well, hopefully this will help," he says, using Tara's remark to introduce his newly acquired client. "Her name is Elaina Haney. I picked her up a few hours before I called you. She told me she had been with Daniel Wade about seven months and she was very happy with him. Then things got complicated."

"Complicated?"

"She wouldn't tell me how, but I have a good idea. You see Tara...Elaina is a Matriarch, and sometimes, things can get complicated with Matriarchs."

"Matriarch," she says, intrigued by the news.

Tara knows Elaina Haney is part of an elite order of erotic dancers at the renowned Night Matriarch, an exclusive men's club of the highest caliber. Its uniqueness is that in a male dominated industry, it's owned and operated exclusively by women. At first, the name was a derogatory slap on the club by the male establishment. In time, the Matriarchs embraced the name, and then used it with resounding success against the establishment.

The status and influence that La Flore's elite personal trainers have with their private training studios is substantial. However, it pales in comparison to the order of Matriarchs. Induction into the highly exclusive covenant is held once every three years as top dancers from across the globe try to gain entry. Twenty were welcomed into the order on its last induction, out of a selection of over a thousand. To be a Matriarch is very demanding but it can be very lucrative. If she plays her cards right, a three-year commitment can render her independently wealthy. A six-year commitment and a Matriarch is a millionaire. What Tara does not know is that the top twenty women recently brought into the order is the most talented pool of dancers in the establishment's history, with Elaina being in the top three of that group.

Tara's expression reveals her thoughts, *"Frank may have given me something very valuable, something that has eluded me for months; a weakness,"* her mind concludes.

"Elaina seems to think Daniel Wade may want to do her harm," he says. "Since their falling out, she never sees him but feels she's being watched. Now she fears for her safety. She refuses to go to the police to avoid more drama since the televangelist scandal they had a year ago. I told her I knew someone who could help. That's when I called you."

Frank hands Tara a glossy business card scented with the faint bouquet of jasmine.

"Ask for Runway and be discrete. She's knows you're coming and is expecting you."

"Thank you, Frank, for everything," Tara says.

"I just want to say…"

"Don't," she interjects with a sweet smile knowing where this is heading. "There is no need to explain or apologize for anything," she says, reaching across the table and grabbing his masculine hands.

"You are and always will be very special to me. Nothing will ever change that. I have to go." The two emerge from the booth and engage in an embrace, much warmer and intimate than the first. After a moment, "Are we friends?" he asks in a meek voice as they continue their embrace.

There is silence. Then in response she gently utters,

"Yes, Frank...We are."

CHAPTER 29

The Night Matriarch

The following day, Tara's drive to The Night Matriarch takes her to La Flore's north side, ten miles past city limits. During the drive, she recalls overhearing comments from Detective Cummins, a staunch patron of men's clubs, about the infamous enterprise. He accompanies his college football roommate, a retired NFL four time pro bowler, since The Night Matriarch is well above Cummins's pay grade. She found it interesting that he never referred to the Matriarchs as dancers the way he did with other clubs.

"There are dancers and then there are Matriarchs," he would boast. She remembers overhearing one story in particular, in which Cummins found himself in a precarious fix.

"So, I have to make this choice you see: turn down a thirty-minute private dance from Firecracker, a fitting name for the hottest Matriarch I had ever laid eyes on, or forego my kid's college money and half my life savings. I'm like, hmm, What to do? What to do? Needless to say, reason and an intervention from my buddy Aaron prevailed at the last minute, but I have to admit, she had me for a moment."

Tara knows Cummins has a flair for exaggeration but knowing him, there is probably some element of truth to his tale.

It is late morning when Tara arrives at what was once a desolate blot on a map. Now, the immense contemporary looking main structure sits on immaculate grounds lightly dotted with alabaster statues of female erotic images. The grounds also highlight an eye-catching marble fountain, similarly adorned. An adjacent building serves as a two story parking garage with a helipad on its roof.

"So, this is the notorious house the Matriarchs built," Tara says, taking in the sights, "Very impressive." To the best of her knowledge, The Night Matriarch is by no means void of scandal but has never been shaken down or accused of engaging in acts of prostitution. However, with its impressive size and ambiance, Tara is incredulous that all she sees before her is derived solely from erotic dancing.

She approaches heavy, well-crafted wooden double doors. Surveillance cameras tell her someone already knows of her presence. Suddenly, one of the doors opens. What stands in the doorway is a bit of a surprise, yet also an enticing sight. *Hmm, I didn't know Frank had a brother*, she thinks, eyeing the six foot two olive skinned security man. The black form-fitting shirt did little to hide his well-built frame.

"Can I help you?" the ruggedly handsome man politely asks in a heavy voice.

"I'm here to see Runway."

"Let her in," a woman's voice says from the intercom mounted next to the door.

Tara follows the man inside to discover, not surprisingly, that the interior was far grander than the exterior.

"Maybe there's more legitimacy to Cummins's tale than I give credit," she thinks. Reaching the large state of the art dance room, her escort stops and listens to his earphone.

"Have a seat here please," he says gesturing her to a plush leather booth.

"Would you like something to drink?" He asks.

"No, thank you."

The man leaves, giving Tara time to take in the surroundings. The modern opulence captivates her. Everything she sees says state of the art, but two features clearly catch her eye. The first is the trademark glass stage with a walkway that extends nearly ninety feet into the main floor, allowing Matriarchs to get up close and personal. The second is a line of doors that display, in gold handsome letters, the stage name of each Matriarch.

"Hmm, the infamous suites. This is where it gets private." Tara tells herself.

A short time later, a casual voice echoes from a distance, "Hello, Detective."

Tara recognizes the voice from the intercom. She lays her sights on a shapely middle-aged brunette approaching her and though extremely attractive, Tara's gut tells her she is not Runway. What clearly resonates about the woman is her demeanor and alluring swagger. Tara finds it strikingly familiar…because it raised her.

"Oh, no need to stand Detective," the woman says as she approaches. She sits in the booth and graciously extends a hand. "I'm Diva, Diva Vaught," she says with a handshake and elegant smile. "And you are?"

"I'm Detective Tara Tanner."

"Well, Detective Tanner, Runway will be here shortly. I hope you are able to help her. We haven't seen talent like hers for some time."

"I have a question about a rumor I'd heard. Maybe you can clarify it for me," Tara says.

"Ask," the woman responds.

"It's my understanding The Night Matriarch is run exclusively by women."

A bright smile takes hold of Diva's face as she lounges back in the booth.

"Ah, the fables continue. We hire men to provide our security, to do the heavy lifting so to speak. After all, they can do more than just help us make babies," Diva says with a lighthearted tone. She sees a shrewd expression on Tara's face.

"Oh, trust me, I'm no feminist," she says, not offended by Tara's look. "There is nothing I enjoy more than the company of a nice man who satisfies."

Diva takes a moment to move closer to Tara. "Detective, this situation needs to be kept under wraps. The media has never been kind to us, if you know what I mean," she says in a pleasant yet sober tone. Tara can see the gravity of Diva's insinuation written on her face.

"I promise. You have my word," she says.

A party of four off duty security men enters the room. They sit at a booth not far from Tara and Diva, eager to embark on their additional and much loved job requirement. The room gradually darkens and Tara begins hearing music. She finally recognizes the song as a female rendition of Prince's "Beautiful One." The song increasingly comes to life. The state of the art sound system delivers the enthralling piece of music with a level of quality Tara had never heard.

"Ah, here she comes now. You could not have timed it better. She's about to trial run her new number," Diva says, gesturing to the large glass stage.

The backdrop of the stage glows a deep red. The black silhouette of a woman, whose lines and curves appear unreal, slowly ascends from the floor piercing the backdrop. Instantly Tara senses a profound shift in the room. Runway's movements are slow and amazingly fluid, evidence of her ballet background. As she performs, it is clear to Tara that she is no ordinary dancer. However, it is the degree of erotic energy she generates through dancing that makes her truly special.

She steps into the light, revealing the other feature needed to enter the fold of Matriarchs. Tara, as fit as her body is, cannot help but to admire what in her eyes, is the perfect balance of muscle firmness, body symmetry and profound erotic femininity. For the first time ever, Tara finds herself thinking,

"If I could look like anyone, it would be her."

As Runway dances, Tara observes what appears to be a tiny, yet distinct scarlet tattoo on her left ankle. She finds it to be an odd accessory for a Matriarch and determines that it must hold some deep significance. Runway's number quickens and brings her close to the two women. Her eyes connect with Tara. The Matriarch's dark blues are piercing and sexual. She sees something in Tara's eyes that prompts a grin. She looks intently at Diva as if waiting for the order to attack. Diva, pleased so far by the performance, gives a sly smile and a slight nod. Runway turns her attention to the four men. Tara grew up seeing this type of influence over men though, never to this extent. In no time, Runway has the four men eating out of her hands. Tara feels such intense sexual energy amongst Runway and just four men that she finds it hard to imagine how much energy is generated with a filled room. Unexpectedly, one of the security men hurriedly retreats to the men's room. Tara looks over at Diva, who grins and subtly gives the unmistakable hand movement addressing her suspicion. Diva then leans over, "Now this is when the money flows," she says softly in Tara's ear.

I can clearly see how things got complicated between Daniel and Elaina. The big question is who, on this side of the Mississippi, could Daniel possibly pick to be Runway's proxy? she asks herself.

Afterwards, Tara enters Elaina's posh private dressing room that smells of jasmine. She finds the blond reclining in a lavish leather chair, sipping a chilled bottled water and looking as if she had just finished a major sporting event.

"That was very impressive," Tara says.

"Thank you," Elaina says with a smile and confident voice.

"You must be the friend Frank told me about."

"Well, that depends on what he told you."

"Don't worry," Elaina says with light laughter, "It was all good. He is a great trainer. I don't need to tell you that. He's quite fond of you and I can see why," she says with a smile.

"I hear Daniel Wade was also a great trainer. At least that's what I was told you said." Elaina's smile fades, bringing a somber look to her face.

"What happened?"

"Well, Detective, everything was great for seven months. Danny,"

"You mean Daniel," Tara responds.

"I call him Danny. It's something just between him and me. He is very good and very professional. A perfectionist, so to speak, and I really liked that. I owe my current conditioning to him." There is a pause, "Then, one night he shows up here during one of my numbers. I didn't think much of it. I even teased him a little. We trained the next day without a mention of the previous night, so I thought it was no big deal. Then he shows up another night...and then another. I was starting to get uncomfortable about the whole thing. What set everything off was the night he saw me after a private dance with one of my clients."

Tara knows a private dance with a Matriarch can easily run thousands of dollars.

"He must have showed up after we'd started. I saw him staring at us walking out of my suite. He appeared calm but I could sense he was furious...and then I felt it."

"Felt what?"

"The other side of him, the side I feel few people know about, and I don't want to know either. I couldn't train with him anymore. With Danny being such a big help and inspiration to me the past seven months, I had to tell him in person. I went to his studio the next day and told him."

"So, you told Daniel you couldn't train with him anymore."

"Yes, I did."

"What happened next?"

"He seemed to take it well. He told me he would reimburse me for the balance of my training via mail and that he was sorry that he caused me any undue stress. I got to my car and realized I left my keys. I went back inside and saw Danny looking as if he was out of sorts. He was pale, sweaty and his eyes were bloodshot. I asked him if he was ok but he was unresponsive, like he was there, but he wasn't. You know? I haven't been back since."

"This is very important," Tara says with a sense of urgency in her voice.

"When did this episode with Daniel occur?"

"About two days ago."

Tara takes a moment to absorb Elaina's story.

"So, you think he's stalking you. What gives you that impression?"

"I think you know," the Matriarch responds with a clever grin.

"Excuse me?"

Elaina gives Tara a look to stop beating around the bush.

"I know you have an intuitive gift, Detective. I saw it in your eyes when I was dancing. I also saw we have similar gifts in other areas," she says in a naughty tone. "For whatever reason, you choose to reject yours while I gladly embrace mine."

"I have no issues with my sexuality if that's what you're implying," Tara asserts.

"I'm sure you don't, at least not on the surface."

Tara's face remains composed, not wanting the Matriarch to know she had hit a nerve; then decides to hit one of her own.

"Speaking of surface, I couldn't help but notice your tattoo, Elaina," she says with a calm yet malicious curiosity. "It threw me at first. Now, I see it's a black widow mark. That's such an odd tattoo for a Matriarch. My gut tells me that it must represent the best of times, the worst of times...or maybe both."

Turns out, Tara's intuition was profoundly accurate. Clyde Anderson, a forty-year-old youthful and charismatic biology professor, taught college freshman Elaina Haney a devastating lesson in love that she would prefer to forget, but knows she never can. Because of his love of arachnids, students around campus simply knew him as...Spider. The tattoo serves as her vow that it will never happen again. An awkward silence engulfs the room. The stunned expression on Elaina's face tells Tara she has hit her mark. The Matriarch feels the sting of her guest hitting a nerve no one else ever has. Rather than have the moment take a turn for the worse, Elaina defuses the situation.

"I'm sorry if I've stepped out of bounds. I didn't mean to offend you in any way. I just feel a kinship between us, and wanted to share it with you. We have a great deal in common, you and I."

Tara lets it go, but an unyielding look tells the Matriarch this meeting is now strictly about business.

"Trust me when I tell you, Detective, I'm afraid my former trainer will harm me or someone else." Quiet blankets the room once more as the two women exchange gazes.

"Thank you, Elaina. You've been a big help." Tara walks to the door and opens it, then stops and turns to face the Matriarch.

"Good luck with your new number; though I have a strong feeling you won't need it." Elaina slowly sits up in her chair, and looks Tara directly in the eyes.

"Good luck with my old trainer. I wish I could say the same about you."

CHAPTER 30

The Standoff

Tara's thoughts are engrossed with Daniel during her drive back to the city. She feels some relief as her gut tells her he has not claimed another victim, but her mind tells her the clock is ticking. *"Finding a proxy for Elaina will be a task that may take Daniel some time, playing to my advantage,"* her mind whispers. Tara knows in order to stop him, she will need help with her surveillance.

Later, she stands at Commander Johnson's desk, "My hands are tied, kiddo," he tells her. "Thanatos has gotten so politically charged by both sides, it's maddening!" he yells, slamming his large hands on his desk. Tara looks at her commander. She refuses to press the issue or show her deep disappointment since she notices his hair, which was salt and pepper months earlier, is now fully gray.

"Stay on Mr. Wade. I will see if I can peel off an extra body to help, but I can't promise you anything."

At 10:00 PM, Tara strolls warily into her den. She knows it is time to address some issues. Earlier, Tara received a phone call from her husband and did not like the tone of his voice when he declared that when she got home, they needed to talk.

Dale is lounging on the plush leather sofa with arms outstretched while Megan lies wide-awake in a fetal position, her head resting on his lap.

"Sunshine, go upstairs…Ok? Mom will be up soon," he says. Megan rises, approaches her mother and gives her a hug. "I'll be up in a bit, baby," Tara says lovingly, caressing her daughter's hair and face. Tara and Dale stare at each other for what seems like an eternity as their daughter strolls upstairs. The looks on their faces speak volumes as they wait to hear the click of her bedroom door. Tara suspected it was a matter of time before this case would take its toll on her family, as it has for the entire city, but the timing could not have been worse.

"Megan is worried about you," Dale says calmly. "She thinks something bad is going to happen to you."

"What do you think, Dale?" Tara asks delicately, knowing she is in no position to be assertive.

"Frankly, I'm a little worried too."

Tara knows without a doubt, Dale has the highest confidence in her ability to take care of herself and is a devoted husband who backs her unconditionally. Rarely has she seen him show concern about her job, and never to this extent. Since they both acknowledge Megan's intuitive gift, Tara feels their daughter's ominous premonition is the fuel stoking her husband's worries.

She walks over to the sofa and gets on both knees between Dale's legs.

"Don't worry, I'll be fine," Tara asserts, caressing his thighs.

"Hmm, let me see," he starts out. "Thanatos is getting all of the media hype, which means most of the resources at Division are focused on him. Now, you know and I suspect Thanatos is bullshit, but since he publicly punked the mayor and chief they have a beef with him. The Democrats see an opportunity to use Thanatos as a political football to get the Mayor's seat in the most bitter election season I've ever seen, anywhere. The sad thing now is this makes Thanatos no longer about justice, but about vendetta and political gain." He pauses for a moment. "Then, we have you." He looks keenly at Tara. "On the fringe of all of this, tailing a man who I strongly suspect is the killer, with no back up from Division. Am I at least in the ball park with this?"

She cannot counter Dale's scenario and refuses to answer. Tara realizes she is at her best when her husband is behind her and knows he is aware that her silence answers his question.

"Tara, you know I'm not the worrying type and I know what it takes to do what you do. I got you into law enforcement remember? In light of what I just said, your reaction to it and Meg feeling something bad is going to happen, how can I not be worried?"

The two stare into each other's eyes. Tara, not in the mood to try to outwit her husband says,

"I remember that handsome officer who got me into law enforcement. I didn't think I had what it took, but he did. He's the reason I made Detective and have come as far as I have." Tara's emotions stir and she feels her eyes stir with tears. "I am able to do what I do simply because you're behind me. Then, there's the Sexton case,"

"The Sexton case was not your fault," Dale interrupts. "Division cleared you of any wrongdoing, so stop beating yourself up over it."

"Let me finish," she says. "You're right, but it was still a very low point in my career. I thought about quitting. Commander Johnson played a part in me staying, but you're the one that inspired me to keep going. Remember what you told me when I expressed to you how I felt like a failure?"

Husband and wife tenderly say together, "Failure is not in falling down, but in staying down."

"That's right," she says as their shared emotions bubble to the surface. "I can't quit now, but I can't do this without you behind me." Tara feels a tear stream down her face.

He looks away. "I'm not behind you, Tara," he says in a solemn tone. He looks his wife in the eyes, "I'm with you. I will always be with you. It's just that I'm a little worried about the well-being of the absolute love of my life. Surely you can understand that."

Tara softly palms and caresses her husband's face. "I understand, and I'd feel the same way if it were you. Don't worry; I have too much to come home to."

The two are locked in a tearful gaze. Tara and Dale come together and engage in a slow, gentle kiss, then another, slightly deeper, and another. Tara stands and straddles Dale sitting on the sofa. Their hands flow freely as they caress each other. Subtle moans begin to fill the room. Tara removes his pullover shirt, displaying his slender athletic torso. He removes her top. They kiss passionately, lips, tongues, teeth roam about the neck, shoulders and chest. Hips, making their distinct motion, further fueling their fervor. Soon, Dale is bursting at the seams, with Tara even more so.

Tara pins Dale's shoulders against the back of the sofa. Frozen in time, they look intently at each other. Engulfed by desire, zippers frantically rip open, belts come off and clothes fall to the floor. She mounts Dale once more. Low groans fill the silence as husband and wife are engrossed in pleasure the instant they enter and receive one another. Their passionate coupling results in an intense mutual orgasm, followed by exhaustion, and collapse.

Later that night, Tara and Dale lie in their bed sound asleep. Tara's rapid eye movement hints at her dream state, as she relives her last stakeout on Daniel's house.

***

It appears routine at first. Tara, as so many other times, peers at the large bay window of the living room. A window shade prevents her from viewing the inside. The interior light illuminates the shade giving the window an eerie amber glow against the night sky. She gets a phone call from her husband who tells her when she gets home they need to talk. Tara hangs up knowing she has issues to confront and that the timing could not have been worse. Tara sets her sights on the bay window once again, and sees something unusual.

For the first time, a shadowy figure stands squarely in the middle of the bay window. To Tara, the figure looks remarkably familiar, taking her back to a previous dream at a time when she was in a desperate search for a killer's identity. Unlike her prior dreams, she knows the identity of the person casting the shadow. What strikes her is that Daniel is facing her as if he knows she is there. Sensing he is trying to intimidate her, and not one for being easily intimidated, Tara gets out of her car, walks into the dark street and faces her shadowy foe with her Glock at the ready, oblivious to the crisp night chill against her skin.

"Make a move…Please," she insists, dark piercing eyes aimed at the dark figure. Then, the shades slowly rise, exposing the man behind them. Tara immediately feels the energy she felt during their appointment, telling her she is in the presence of the other Daniel Wade. She sees the face is not the Daniel she remembers. His face, his eyes in particular, harbors a sinister presence that makes him look almost unrecognizable.

Tara knows the evil staring at her was the last thing Kelly Vogel, Cedric Wells and the rest of his victims ever saw. She is determined that there will not be another, since his next proxy may suffer a far worse fate than Jessica Stoval. She recognizes this is Daniel's moment to take full advantage of La Flore's frenzy over Thanatos. She sees he is emboldened enough to reveal his other side in plain sight, sending her a blatant message, "I know you're alone."

The clear chilly night ends with Tara and Daniel in a standoff, aware that they are the only players in this potentially deadly game.

***

Tara emerges from her sleep assured of one thing. For one of them, this game, without question, will end tragically.

CHAPTER 31

The Chase

It is midmorning at a bustling Division when Detective Cummins walks in and heads directly to Commander Johnson's office accompanied by a middle-aged portly woman. Her stature is less than five-feet, making keeping up with Detective Cummins's long strides arduous at best. Her dark ringed eyes remain fixed to the floor as she refuses to look about. Occasionally, she runs her hand through thinning hair. Some of the detectives recognize the woman as one of the clerks in Records Division. As they make their way through the commotion, the two catch the eye and curiosity of Detective McVey. Cummins looks over at McVey and gestures him to follow. As he walks by Tara's desk, Cummins takes a long stare at the vacant space. The commander, in the middle of a phone conversation, sees the party approaching his door. The three finally converge on his doorway with the two detectives towering over the woman. Johnson waves to the three to enter.

"Hey, something important has come up. I'll call you back."

As the commander hangs up, Cummins closes the door behind him. In an abrupt tone he says, "Commander Johnson, I think you need to hear this."

Meanwhile, Tara is well into her stakeout of Daniel. From the onset, she noticed a significant change in his pattern. Not wearing his training garb, Daniel is wearing jeans and a plain, dark colored t-shirt, blending in with La Florians. Tara trails Daniel from his home to his training studio. She notices Becky's car in the parking lot as Daniel enters the studio. After some time, he emerges with a gym bag and walks to his car. There, he stops and looks around. For a brief moment, he stares in Tara's direction before tossing the bag in the back seat and getting in his car. Tara fires up the engine, "Well, this is it," she says.

The two drive off with Tara locked on Daniel as they begin to cruise through the late morning traffic. Time passes as they journey towards La Flore's Lower East Side. Once there, they find themselves at The Village, a large neighborhood of various modest apartments. Daniel enters the Peak Apartment's parking area. Tara parks at a nearby apartment complex that only allows her to observe the Peak's entry and exit.

A short time later, Daniel's car reappears. As he exits the parking area, Tara notices that he has a passenger. Her senses go on high alert when she sees the blonde woman sitting on the passenger side. As she attempts to follow, busy oncoming traffic stalls her. Not wanting to give away her position, Tara waits impatiently as she watches Daniel's car fade from view. Finally, she mounts her enforcement light on the roof of the car with its brilliant flash getting an immediate response from the traffic. Her engine revs as she hurries onto the busy street. Quickly, she retrieves her light from the roof and streaks to find Daniel.

Tara scans the area for clues. Growing up on the Lower East Side, she knows this particular street has many intersections and that he could have taken any one of them. Several minutes pass with no luck in her search. She hurriedly combs the area, going from one intersection to another, looking for signs of him. For Tara, quitting now is definitely not an option. She knows a life is on the line and her failure to find Daniel will mean a certain and cruel death for his unsuspecting passenger.

"C'mon, c'mon," she says intently under her breath, pounding her steering wheel.

"Where the hell are you?"

Nearly forty minutes pass before Tara has a stroke of luck. Crossing a bridge over an interstate, she spots Daniel's car cruising on the slow moving highway. In an instant, tires squeal and the engine roars as she breaks for the interstate. Knowing her former neighborhood the way she does, Tara quickly makes an easy work of curves, turns and light traffic. She gets on a road running adjacent to the interstate. The road's higher elevation provides her with a bird's eye view of the highway. In the distance, she can see Daniel's car amidst the traffic.

Tara realizes she has to get to the interstate before Daniel reaches the next major junction. Once there, he would be nearly impossible to find. Less than a quarter of a mile from the highway entrance, Tara speeds past a black and white patrol car. "Shit!" she blurts as flashing lights suddenly illuminate and the menacing looking vehicle comes barreling towards her. Tara does not stop but slows down. The patrol car swiftly veers and pulls up beside her. The officer lowers his window and signals Tara to pull over. Tara looks again upon the interstate and sees Daniel's car approaching a junction.

Tara rolls down her window to expose her detective's badge palmed in her hand. The officer examines the badge as it shines in the sunlight. Tara glances once again upon the interstate then hastily looks over at the officer. After a moment, the officer gives Tara a nod and backs away. Tara slams the throttle while eyeing the freeway entrance sign. She enters onto the interstate at breakneck speed. She quickly swerves across to the fast lane, which, to her relief, is void of traffic. Tara whisks past cars as she speeds to catch Daniel before he reaches the next junction. She catches sight of another patrol car that she swiftly passes. Tara's car is a bullet as it is traveling well over one hundred miles an hour. For once, her focus is not on Daniel, but on avoiding a wipeout that would cover a substantial chunk of interstate. The junction rapidly comes into Tara's sight, just in time for her to see Daniel's car veer off onto Exit East 135 to Old Highway 77. Suddenly, a Nissan unaware of her fast approaching car, veers into her lane from behind the blind spot of a semi. Once there, the driver has only milliseconds to react as it assesses a potentially catastrophic predicament and quickly swerves back into its previous lane, missing Tara by millimeters. The screeching of tires from the

Nissan and a thunderous blast from the horns of the semi is all that resulted from the nearly disastrous encounter. Tara finally arrives at the exit and onto Old Highway 77. She can see Daniel's car in the distance. Knowing there are no exits or junctions for miles, she is content to keep her distance.

Several minutes pass as the two casually cruise the nearly deserted highway. Tara's gut tells her Daniel's destination is old Sleater Thomas Industrial Park, condemned for many years. Her suspicion is confirmed when she sees him turn off onto Sleater Thomas Road. The one lane thoroughfare winds and meanders over wooded hilly terrain. Soon, the highway, the city of La Flore and civilization disappear. Tara has lost sight of Daniel, but in her gut, she knows that the abandoned park is his ultimate destination. She turns onto a side road and after a few feet, meets a weathered metal fence. The rusty, and ominous looking "Danger! Do Not Enter" sign mounted on the battered gate, stares at Tara as if giving her a stern warning.

Tara, undeterred by the sign, eases out of her car and into the clear afternoon sunlight. With a quick glance, she notices the heavy lock and rusted chain were simply window dressing, merely wrapped around the fence post. She sees the lock on the bundle of chain is cut. What strikes her is that the cut on the lock was clearly not recent. She assesses the lock had been cut no less than several months ago. Victim Kelly Vogel flashes to mind as her body was discovered on Old

Highway 77. Tara has a strong hunch that Daniel may have killed the victim here. She unravels the chain and then opens the gate before getting back into her car.

The drive a few feet beyond the gate reveals ten large abandoned buildings comprised of manufacturing plants, wholesale buildings and warehouses. To Tara, the area is massive, well isolated and to her knowledge, has no history of any illegal activity.

The cruel images of Jessica Stoval flash in her head as she cruises the park in her car, intensely scanning each building. The voice of Dr. Russell rings loud as she recalls his gruesome details of Jessica's injuries. *"What was done to her took a while,"* her mind hears the doctor say.

Tara sees the image of Daniel's blonde proxy sitting in his passenger seat. Her opinion is that there could be no better place than here to act upon whatever insidious and monstrous fantasy Daniel may have planned.

As she clears one of the large buildings, Tara spots Daniel's car parked by an entrance to one of the manufacturing plants. She slams the gas pedal, shooting towards the ominous looking building. Once there, she assesses Daniel's car and her predicament.

"Ok, what the hell am I going to do for backup?" she asks herself. Wanting to keep her commander away from any liability in case something goes wrong, she refrains from calling him. Operating under the radar, outside

Division protocols and feeling pressed for time to save Daniel's hostage, she retrieves her cell phone, and then dials.

***

"This is Agent Jenkins of LFPD's Background and Intelligence Division. I am currently away from my desk but if you leave your name, the time and a detailed message after the beep, I will get back to you as soon as possible. Thank you and have a great day."

"Agent Jenkins, this is Detective Tanner. I am at the Sleater Thomas Industrial Park at building 1025 in pursuit of secondary suspect Daniel Wade. Suspect has a hostage and believed next victim. Hostage is a blonde female. Suspect and hostage are inside the building. Suspect is believed to be armed and dangerous, and the hostage is believed to be under duress. I am about to enter the building and pursue the suspect. You've always come through for me. Maybe you can come through again." There is a pause followed by a much softer tone, "Agent Jenkins…Thanks, girlfriend…for everything."

CHAPTER 32

Circumstance … Terminal

Tara's adrenaline rises and her heart races. Taking a deep breath, she stares at the rusted metal door from her car. Grabbing her Glock, chambering a round and bringing an extra clip for good measure, she gets out of her car and dons the vest from her trunk before heading to the door. Tara holds her weapon with arms extended and aiming low. Taking cover by standing to the side, her free hand carefully turns the doorknob. Finding it unlocked, she pulls forcefully, swinging it open while still maintaining her cover.

The door swings freely, banging against a wall. The afternoon sun beams through the entrance, illuminating some of the building's shadowy interior. Tara darts her head repeatedly, peeking inside. Feeling confident, she enters the building, finding herself in a large room. Using the shadows for concealment and allowing her eyes to adjust to the dim natural lighting, she scans the room and sees an open doorway. Making her way to the entrance, she takes cover on one side. She darts her head in the doorway, peeking at what appears to have been the main manufacturing floor.

A large piece of heavy machinery, left on the main floor a few feet away, appears to be good cover. She sprints to the structure, keeping a low profile and in short order, rests next to the dense metal. Tara looks around and hastily inventories the main floor. From above hang lifeless overhead cranes. To her left and several yards away is a row of large observation windows and a metal double door. To her right and at equal distance, there are three large bay doors to loading docks. Tara's head snaps back towards the observation windows upon hearing a frightful scream.

Without hesitation, Tara is in a dead sprint towards the observation windows, knowing the open distance to travel makes her an easy target. The adrenalin surge prompted by the scream proves to be highly beneficial as Tara, despite the weight of her vest, covers the area much faster than anticipated. She feels Daniel is probably too occupied with whatever insidious act he is doing to his hostage. Tara finally reaches the metal double door.

From behind the entrance, a violent commotion rages. Tara pulls the door open and enters, aiming her weapon. The uproar is loud, coming from one of the back offices. She heads in that direction and feels Daniel's energy on a plane much more sinister and profound than their last encounter. *He's here*, her mind confirms.

"Why are you doing this to me?" yells a distraught voice clearly in tears and pain.

"Shut up," returns a heavy voice and the distinct sound of a vicious slap.

Tara quickly hones in on the office door from where the commotion emanates. She rushes to the door, eager to unload her Glock. The force from her kick nearly takes the flimsy wooden door off its hinges.

Tara crashes into the room and takes aim. What she sees next stuns her, sending her weapon falling down to her side, suspended in a feeble grip. The flat screen mounted on the wall shows Daniel beating Jessica Stoval mercilessly. She is bound to a chair and salivates as her nose runs with a mixture of fluids.

"Oh, we're just getting started," he replies in a menacing tone. "You'll pay for that little stunt you pulled in my office, Complete Bitch."

The victim slowly lifts her head, showing an already swollen face. "I told you," she says through slurred speech and streams of tears. "You've got the wrong person. I'm not a detective. I don't want to die."

Tara eyes her proxy staring at her from the large flat screen. Still fixed on the screen, a stir snaps Tara out of her daze. Her eyes narrow and the hairs on the back of her neck stand up. She gently clenches her weapon and prepares to move. Tara remains calm as her senses warn that Daniel is present, stalking, directly behind her and closing in. Both patiently wait for each other to come within range. Now, it is hard to determine who is predator, and who is prey. When the moment is right, they both strike. Like a viper, Daniel lunges forward. With amazing quickness, Tara raises her weapon over her shoulder and fires a blind shot behind her, then turns to unload the rest of the lethal cargo.

Midway through her turn, she feels a vise-like grip around her firing hand. Another hand, holding a rag,

254

goes over her mouth and nostrils. Tara quickly finds herself in a python-like clinch and unable to move. She stops breathing to avoid inhaling the wet substance on the rag, she feels against her skin.

"Now, now," Daniel says. "Just let it go. C'mon...you can do it."

Time passes as she fights frantically to break Daniel's hold. With her body now screaming for air, she desperately struggles to avoid breathing. With no other recourse, Tara gives in. She gasps heavily, filling her lungs with fumes from the fast acting drug soaked on the rag.

"There, that a girl," he says tenderly. "See, that didn't hurt a bit."

It does not take long before the highly efficient drug takes effect. She gradually loosens the grip on her Glock as her body relaxes and eyelids become heavy. There is a heavy "ca-thud" as the weapon hits the floor. Blurred vision reveals her proxy staring at her from the flat screen as if to say, "I wish I could help you." Finally, Tara's sight goes black as she slips into unconsciousness in Daniel's arms. With his voice in demonic distortion, the last thing she hears is, "Nighty-night, Sweet Princess,"

From the darkness, the cement floor comes into focus. Tara is starting to get her wits about her. She finds herself alone, bound to a sturdy wooden chair in a dimly lit room from an overhead light. Windows, thickly coated with years of grunge, repel the afternoon sunlight. Tara challenges her bonds. Resistance is futile. As the drug continues to wear off, she looks about, taking in her surroundings. The limited light in the spacious near empty room allows Tara to make out the few objects around her. She notices a flimsy wooden table a few feet in front of her. On the table lays the gym bag she recalls Daniel carrying to his car. Tara can see there are other objects laying on the table and though she cannot make them out, knows they are not for good intensions. Observing the object placed under the table, the shape of the container with its cargo of gasoline is unmistakable.

The desolate aura of the room further drives home the isolation she feels. Then, a thought strikes her. She pauses for a moment, realizing she is not wearing the same clothes. Assessing her newly acquired apparel, she does not like what she sees. Black stiletto pumps, black stockings and the black leather two-piece outfit is a foreboding sign. The smell of jasmine fills her nostrils. Upon detecting the fragrance, Tara recalls where she last encountered the floral scent.

"Frank's a great trainer. I don't need to tell you that. He's quite fond of you and I can see why," were the kind words of the Matriarch.

She stubbornly rejects her mind's ominous conclusion despite overwhelming proof. Something catches the corner of her eye. Hesitantly, she turns her head to look over her right shoulder. Staring at the dusty pane glass leaning against a wall shattered all doubts and denials of her dilemma. The reflection of the blonde bound to the chair, staring back at her, answers her question about who is the unfortunate soul to be the Matriarch's proxy. Her stomach knots and panic follows as the grim reality sets in. Tara knows without a doubt, that her hours are numbered and her circumstance…terminal.

CHAPTER 33

Slipping Into Fantasy

Tara hears someone approaching from behind. She turns her head as Daniel strolls around to face her. Once in front of her, Tara sees a large gauze bandage covering one side of his face, along his cheek and lower ear. He looks at her for a moment and then carefully removes the bloodstained gauze. He turns his face to display the shallow scar that runs along his entire cheek, ending at a small missing piece of earlobe.

"This is definitely going to leave a mark," he says, looking at her. "Clever shot. A lesser man wouldn't have seen that coming, couldn't have evaded it, and would be dead now."

Fully recovered from the drug she says, "Not clever enough."

In light of her newly acquired apparel, her stare asks a pressing question.

"No, I didn't fuck you if that's what you're wondering," he says. "Besides, that's not my style. I'll admit, you're quite the specimen, and I suspect when you came to me, you already had a trainer."

Tara finds no comfort in Daniel's claim or his accolade.

"What about the blonde I saw in your car earlier?"

"Who…Ash?" he asks with a grin.

"You should have guessed by now. She was merely a decoy. An old client I was helping with a lift, but it worked beautifully. I figured you'd be so focused on rescuing my friend that you would fail to realize you were the mark all along. Except for my little...souvenir," he says, gently touching his fresh wound, getting blood on the tips of his fingers. "It turned out much better than I expected. So, here we are. No hostage...Just you and me."

He examines the blood on the tip of his finger before rubbing it between finger and thumb.

"Do you want to know what happened at the office that day with Elaina? Do you want to know how I...killed the Matriarch?"

Tara remains silent, not particularly interested in knowing the details of what Daniel has in store for her.

"Well, I'm going to tell you anyway," he says shrewdly, casually pacing. "I beat her savagely, then violated her with several abrasive objects. I mutilated her face and body with hundreds of cuts with a razor. She wrenched in agonizing pain as I doused her with gasoline, letting the corrosive fluid settle into her exposed wounds. Finally, I set her ablaze and watched her fight frantically as the flames consumed her, reducing her to charred remains. A fitting end for a Matriarch," he stops and faces her, "Don't you think?"

Disturbed by Daniel's horrid scenario, she sees him drifting further and further away with each passing moment of recalling his attack. He is slipping into fantasy. She realizes her proxy's fate was sealed the instant Daniel saw her as Detective Tanner. Feeling she has even less time, Tara has to figure out how to deal with him once he sees her as Elaina. In an attempt to keep him in reality she says, "I found your message in Jessica's wallet."

He chuckles. "I knew you would find it. That's why I can never underestimate you," he says, looking her squarely in the face.

"What happened at SEAL school, Daniel?" Tara asks in an attempt to reach him and buy more time. "Why did you wash out a week before graduating when you were third in your class? Why do your records state "psychological reasons"? You have no criminal record. Your clients love you, and I sense that deep down you are a good man. Something has to be wrong for a person out of nowhere..." Tara stops. Nevertheless, she sees Daniel get the message. He stands motionless, wearing a stony expression she finds hard to read.

"Look, I believe whatever happened to you isn't your fault. You may have a strong defense case and the courts can clear you of any wrongdoing. I can help you, Daniel. Please let me help you."

He stands motionless. Tara sees a look signifying her words are getting through. Then, she sees his skin turn pale and clammy and the blood vessels in his eyes dilate, giving them a crimson hue. Daniel faces away from her and walks to the table a few feet away. With arms stretched out along the wooden structure, he lowers his head. Tara feels uneasiness about the change of events. He slowly raises his head.

"You shouldn't have let me see you like that...Elaina," he says in a calm but firm tone. "Do you enjoy dancing for them, their hands all over you?"

Tara's stomach knots as she realizes Daniel is no longer in reality. Making matters worse, she is clueless how to respond to her bleak dilemma. He turns his head and looks over his shoulder.

"Answer me," he says.

Tara remains frozen and helpless. Getting no response, he rushes over, grabs her by the chin and lifts it with a strong hand, forcing her to look up at him.

"Don't get me started...Matriarch."

She looks up into forceful, intimidating eyes. Upon looking deeper, Tara sees her answer. Daniel slowly draws his face closer, as if to kiss her. Instead, he gently runs his nose along her face and neck. Hearing the rush of wind through his nostrils, Tara knows he is taking in the jasmine scent. He pauses, projects a threatening look at her before gently releasing his grip, returning to the table with his back to her. He lowers his head and closes his eyes.

"I wasn't dancing for them, Danny. I was dancing for you."

Impulsively, his eyes open and head snaps up. There is quiet. Tara's heart hammers for what seems like an eternity, waiting to see if her gamble has paid off.

"Don't play games with me, Elaina," he says in a hostile tone.

"I'm not playing games," Tara replies.

Watching Daniel moments earlier, she sees he is at odds with himself about Elaina. She knows his initial urge is to make her pay a horrific price for triggering his last attack. The answer she saw in his eyes had to do with his feelings towards the Matriarch. Tara didn't know whether she saw Daniel's love or infatuation for her, but was sure she saw a lifesaving opportunity that she was not about to pass up. To pull it off, Tara realizes she must embrace the part of her she vowed never to accept; the part of her in which the Matriarch felt a kinship; the part of her that could break her husband the way she felt it broke her father; the part of her that was her mother.

"I waited for you, but you didn't show up. What was I to do?" she asks.

Tara waits nervously for a reply, as Daniel remains motionless.

"There was an accident and I was stuck in traffic," he murmurs.

"Danny, what I did was my job," she says softly. "Had you been there it would never have happened."

263

As she pauses, something starts to stir within her. "I had just gotten into my dance when I finally saw you. I knew you were very upset. I could see it in your eyes. You were too upset to notice what was truly going on." Daniel turns to face Tara wearing an unreadable expression. "After I saw you, I was trying to show you that this is what I would do...if we were alone."

"Then why come to me the next day to end it? Why go train with this, Frank Perrino guy? Are you two hitting it off? Is the pretty boy fucking you?" He stops for a moment. "I'm...I'm sorry...That didn't come out right."

"First of all," Tara says in a calm but firm tone, "Frank's gay. Secondly, I was afraid."

"Afraid of what! That someone would get hurt?"

Upon seeing him become agitated, Tara knows she must remain calm.

"I think you know," she says.

She looks at him, now comfortable in her role. "Correct me if I'm wrong, but I know you have feelings for me. There are things a woman just knows."

She can see Daniel is at war with himself, that part of this super predator thinks the matter is folly and nothing more than a desperate attempt to avoid a violent and torturous death, yet part of him is captivated and cannot help but to hear out her affectionate words, which are having the effect of Kryptonite.

"If I had stayed, things would have gotten complicated. You see, I'm bound by oath from having feelings for anyone, let alone having a relationship, especially with my trainer. Yes, I was afraid someone would get hurt, but not the way that you were thinking. I was beginning to feel a conflict, about being a Matriarch, about being with you. When I saw how angry you had gotten, I knew you felt the same. In life, there are things we want to do and then there are things we have to do. I saw where this was going and as much as I wanted to stay, I had to leave…so neither one of us would get hurt."

Tara feels a peculiar aura about the room. Not the pure sinister form she had felt earlier, but an antagonistic mix of energies that has Daniel stunned for the moment. Tara knows her efforts, though effective so far, are only temporary, and that her life rests solely on getting free of her bonds and escaping from, capturing or killing Daniel.

Realizing she has the upper hand, "Danny," she says with a hint of naughtiness, "Remember when you first came to see me?"

There is silence. Tara knows to lose her composure now would be fatal.

"Yes, I remember," he responds as if in mild hypnosis.

"Remember how I looked at you the way you were looking at me? I never told you how much fun that was when we trained the next day, and I was curious why you didn't mention anything. Did you not enjoy our time together?"

After a moment, "I was ashamed."

"Ashamed? Of what?"

"Ashamed of what I did when I got home," he says.

"Well, as long as you were thinking about me, about us, then there's nothing to be ashamed of. Now that I know you did enjoy our time together, you're going to love what I have to say next."

Tara gets a look from Daniel but knows it is in anticipation of what she is insinuating.

"I have a number I made up, just for you. Do you want to see it?"

Realizing Daniel remains enthralled, she completely immerses herself in the Matriarch's role.

"It's a number with a little...Southern charm."

Tara takes a deep breath and closes her eyes. In that instant, she breaks her lifelong vow. There is no paranormal event, no spirits, nothing like that; but releasing her mother was as natural as breathing. When she gradually exhales, opens her eyes and looks at Daniel, she possesses the stare, erotic charm and seductive voice of the person she swore never to become, not knowing by letting this genie out of the bottle, whether she will be able to put it back.

"I know you want to see the number I made for you, and underneath that...sinister demeanor, I know you'd like nothing more than to fuck my brains out. As much as I'd love to experience both, I'm afraid it would be quite difficult, with me bound to this chair."

CHAPTER 34

Out of Time

Tara sees skepticism in Daniel. Undeterred, her eyes say he is in for the time of his life. She looks nonchalantly at her bonds, before casting her mother's glare back at him.

"What's the problem?" she asks with a grin. "Surely a big, strong stud like you can handle little ol' me. Trust me, you can handle me anyway you'd like."

Daniel moves towards her, and then hesitates. She sees he still has the wits about him to put her charade under scrutiny. However, her seduction proves to be too much for him as it soon overpowers any doubt.

Daniel has become victim to the very reason Tara was his mark from the beginning. There were a number of blonde women he could have chosen as Elaina's proxy, from a physical standpoint. However, the Matriarch's intangible persona is what marked Tara, a persona that she too possesses.

He approaches, and begins removing her bonds, starting with her legs.

"Uh uh…slower," she says.

Daniel stops and looks Tara in the face, then succumbs to her request.

"That's it. That's how to undress me."

Daniel removes the bonds from shapely legs, and then caresses them.

"You have beautiful legs," he says.

"I'm glad you like them."

He begins removing the bonds around her torso. He pauses. The two engage in a close stare, feeling the warmth of each other's breath. He undoes the bond tied loosely over her breast. Strong hands gently touch them.

"Mmm, now that's the spot," she says. "Well, at least one of them."

The heat from her body releases the jasmine scent as her seductive prowess is now equal to, if not greater than Elaina's. Daniel continues to loosen the bonds until both arms are unbound, and Tara is free.

She stands, grabs Daniel by the shirt and swings him around, shoving him into the chair. In no time, he sits with her straddling him. She pins both his shoulders with arms extended against the back of the chair. Pulling herself close to him, she brings her breast within an inch of his face, exposing him to more of the intoxicating scent. She whispers in his ear, "Relax, I have something special for you."

Tara gets up and with a confident swagger, strolls towards the table. She finds herself gazing upon a menacing blade; abrasive objects varied in sizes and a disposable lighter. Her nose catches a subtle whiff of the flammable fluid from the half-gallon container sitting underneath the table. Briefly, her nerves are challenged, but unwavering as she stands facing the ominous display. She feels she is at a crossroads and senses this is as good a time as any to move against her captor, but the woman she embraced moments earlier has other plans. She turns to face him. Watching him stare…spellbound. Her mother's smile takes hold of her face as she strolls back toward the chair. She stops short, and starts her dance.

Flashes of a plethora of memories and imagery flood her thoughts. Runway's performance at The Night Matriarch mingles with nonstop visions of her mother's innumerable conquests of young prey. Her mother's words echo as Tara remembers the dream of seeing her, insatiably ravaged by Frank, moments before an intense orgasm.

"Tara, I'm going to be detained for a moment, girl stuff, you know how it is."

The graphic images and sounds of lust and sex are vivid, deafening and as rich in her conscious as the music during Runway's performance. Her efforts pay off as channeling her mother, her dance and the body her trainer Frank built, transforms Tara's performance into an erotic firestorm. Her vision takes her to an open men's bathroom stall where she witnesses the security guard from the Night Matriarch groan as he erupts uncontrollably, releasing himself. Diva approaches her with the look of approval. "Bravo Detective. Bravo. Seems your mother is a woman after my own heart," she says, softly clapping her hands. Upon reaching Tara, Diva utters in her ear, "Now this is when the money flows."

Tara knows she has Daniel and feels his ever-mounting desire for her. Realizing she must act, Tara scans the room looking for a means to deal with him. She finds her answer when her sights catch the thin leather straps that earlier served as her bonds, piled around his feet.

Tara approaches him and kneels between his legs to retrieve a strap. Her hands grasp and skillfully fondle Daniel's erection, protruding through his jeans. She brings her mouth within centimeters of his pulsing organ.

"Elaina," he gasps, as the tease of oral sex has him moaning at the prospect. Tara cautiously grabs a leather strap from the floor. Daniel's head collapses back with his eyes closed and neck exposed. She leisurely gets up. Her free hand gently caresses his chest, arms and shoulders as she strolls behind him. By the time she is in position, both ends of the strap are wrapped firmly around her hands as her face morphs to Tara's more serious look, a look with lethal intentions.

Her strike is immediate, forceful and precise. Daniel bolts from the chair with frantic hands unable to free his neck from the rigid choke hold blocking his airway. As he stands, Daniel exposes his back. Instantly, Tara jumps on and wraps powerful legs around his waist, putting him in a python clinch. He backs into a wall and repeatedly bashes her body against the concrete structure. She knows to lose her grip would be suicide, and holds on for dear life.

Daniel continues his relentless battering, bruising Tara's back and shoulders. His hands reach back and blindly attempt to grab hair or gouge an eye. He desperately tries to head butt her nose and face. Asphyxiating sounds become more and more apparent with each passing moment. His legs buckle. Tara senses he is feeling the effects of her assault. Daniel pounds frantically on her legs with hammer fists and elbows strikes. She grimaces from pain and exhaustion but holds on steadfastly. He staggers towards the table, stopping just beyond arm's reach. Tara stares at the blade lying on the table and knows she cannot allow him to reach it, but feels she has nothing left. It is as if the years of fatigue and pain during the brutal sessions with her trainer Frank, prepared her for this precise moment.

"Remind me why I do this again."

"You never know what you may encounter that will require this level of training."

She hears his imposing voice when during a session, she was about to quit. *If you won't do it for yourself, do it for me!*

The muscles of Tara's arms and legs constrict, applying greater force to the strap around Daniel's neck and the clinch around his waist.

She feels his legs start to give way. He falls to his knees. Daniel is seconds from passing out but somehow manages to get back to his feet in a final attempt to escape.

Sensing he is about gone, Tara whispers in his ear, "Nighty-night, Sweet Prince."

Daniel hurls both legs high off the floor, leaving Tara's back exposed to receive the brunt of the impact as the two plummet toward the concrete floor.

She is fortunate that Daniel's desperate attempt put them over the sturdy wooden table. Tara, falling along with nearly two hundred pounds of Daniel, proved too much for the wooden structure. They easily crash through the table, hurling the objects and scattering them about the floor. The table did much to prevent Tara from breaking her back, but that was it. Upon hitting the floor, Tara lets go a piercing yell as well as her grip, the wind knocked out of her. Daniel rolls over and frees his neck from the strap, coughing violently. For a brief time, they both try to recover from their arduous ordeal. Withstanding the worst of the fall has weakened an already exhausted Tara. She lies on the floor, then looks over to see Daniel slowly stagger to his feet.

His expression tells her he has gotten more than what he had bargained for, as he looks ragged. His head and eyes wander about as he scans for his blade. He finally spots it in a corner a few feet away and in light of recent events, she feels he is now resolved to making his kill a quick one. He slowly stumbles to retrieve it.

Tara is resigned, feeling she has played all of her cards and has given it her best shot. She comes to peace with her fate.

She thinks of Megan, Sara and Dale; of fond days as a little girl spent with her father, picking blackberries in the holly. *She stands in a lush field under clear skies, face to face with her mother.*

"We almost did it, didn't we Momma?"

"Yes, Tara, we almost did," her mother replies lovingly.

They reach out to each other. Their hands form a soft clinch for the first time, as the cold reflective barrier separating them for years, is gone.

After a moment, "Thank you...for trying to help."

She returns to the present and sees Daniel, standing in the corner, holding the frightening blade. Neither her mother nor the Matriarch can save her now. She is out of time.

"You betrayed me again. It was all a lie, a game, wasn't it," he says in a hostile tone. "Now, I have a game. It's called how many stabs does it takes to kill a Matriarch."

Daniel gets a firm stabbing grip on the blade and walks deliberately toward Tara. He kneels over her. She projects a defiant face, void of fear. "Time to die, Elaina."

Daniel raises his arm to deliver his first blow. Suddenly, there is a deafening crash and thunderous rumble.

"Freeze!" comes a commanding yell. Daniel can see scores of laser light beams honed on him in the darkness.

"Move away Mr. Wade! Drop the knife and get down on the floor! Do it!"

Daniel looks at Tara, staring back at him. "Mr. Wade! Drop the knife and get down or we'll shoot!"

Daniel looks up again to see the myriad of lasers. The spectral sight induces a flashback of the vivid dream he had about Elaina and Tara, a dream that now seems more a premonition that has finally come to fruition. He looks down again. For an instant, Tara looks into eyes that are tired of fighting whatever demons caused him to commit such atrocities, eyes that long to be free.

"Mr. Wade! Put the weapon down!"

Lying flat on the floor, Tara removes the blonde wig, exposing her dark hair. She looks at him.

"The fantasy is over, Daniel. Let me help you."

He looks at her, "You can't."

He raises his blade to deliver his blow. The light beams instantly disappear from the brilliant flash of muzzles. Before Daniel can deliver a downward swing, the deadly swarm of bullets, accompanied by a shockwave, hit their mark. They make quick work of his fit frame, ripping through flesh, rupturing organs and shattering bones. Tara has the ultimate seat in the house, hearing rounds whiz just inches above her. The heavy thudding sounds of bullets hitting their target are too many and too rapid for her to count. The lethal volley has Tara seeing Daniel riddled with lead, spraying her with a mist of blood, before hurtling him three feet away.

Tara lies in the wreckage of wood, speckled with blood.

Soaking in all that just happened; she realizes it is just a matter of time before her adrenaline subsides.

"Man, I'm sure as hell going to be sore tomorrow," she laments, staring at the ceiling.

Tara sees Detectives Cummins and McVey standing over her.

"Tanner, you ok?" Cummins asks, in a rare display of worry.

"Yeah, help me up."

She grabs Cummins's hand. As she stands, her muscles give hint to her prognosis.

"Where's the hostage?" McVey asks.

"No hostage."

McVey and Cummins glance at each other, slightly taken aback by the news.

Tara is handed a large midnight blue department jacket with bold gold letters, LFPD written on the back. Looking around, she sees the area abuzz with activity. She looks over her shoulder and observes a paramedic cover Daniel's body with a sheet. She takes a moment to stare at the figure lying on the dusty concrete floor. Tara faintly limps outside into the clear night with Detective Cummins to find the abandoned industrial park ablaze with the blue flashing lights of what appears to be the entire department. She hears the chopping blades of helicopters hovering overhead, their powerful searchlights scouring the area. Approached by a paramedic, she only asks for a towel. Cummins points her in the direction of the black Crown Victoria, parked beyond the bustle. He escorts her through the commotion and into the back seat of the car. There, she sits next to a calm Commander Johnson.

"Yeah, Commander," Cummins starts out, "Caught her lying down on the job again as usual. I didn't get the memo that today was casual Thursday. I have a smoking Chippendale outfit I've been dying to wear," he says through the open rear window.

Tara knows she's fine when her mind conjures, "I can't imagine what's worse, my ordeal with Daniel, or that visual."

"Good night, Detective," the commander says, using a power button, closing the tinted window.

The two gaze outside at the activity, now muffled by the glass.

"Where's the hostage?" he asks.

Tara remains silent.

"There was no hostage," she replies.

"Hmm, let me guess, there was no hostage because you were the proxy…am I right?"

Her silence as she stares out the window more than answers his question.

"After all these years, I never thought I'd see another case like this. At least the good guys won this time," he says.

"I don't know," Tara says in a thoughtful tone, thinking about the look in Daniel's eyes in his final moments…

"What do you mean, you don't know?"

After a moment, "Nothing," she says, shaking her head.

"Do you know who you were the proxy for, by chance?"

"No," she answers, keeping her vow to Diva.

"Well, it doesn't matter," he responds. "You did well today, kiddo. All that's important now is that you're ok.

Have the medics check you out, then get cleaned up and go home to Dale and Megan. You can write your report in the morning."

Go home to Dale and Megan, her mind reflects. That's never sounded so good.

"I take it Agent Jenkins got my message," she asks, holding the blood stained towel, curious about the department's apparent overkill and seeming complete disregard for Thanatos.

"Yes, she did, but that doesn't explain everything you see."

Tara looks outside, observing a news helicopter hovering nearby. She looks at her commander. "Care to fill me in?"

CHAPTER 35

The Interesting Piece

'*W*e *provide local news like no one else…period! This is KAPO 7 news with Anchorwoman, Ashley Craig. Today, our follow-up edition on Thursday's breaking news of how the LFPD finally prevails and an elusive killer is dead. Here's your host Ashley Craig."*

Good afternoon. The terror that has gripped our city for over a year ended as last Thursday night, police gunned down the killer. Like a suspenseful murder mystery, this story has…some twists and turns. The killer turns out not to have been Thanatos at all, but more on that story later. The major question is why would Daniel Wade, a person with no criminal history, a distinguished record of service to his community and his country and loved by his clients and associates turn out to be a vicious killer? That answer…we may never know. With Daniel Wade being the real killer, the next question is…Who is Thanatos? That answer came Thursday morning as a tip from Serena Lofton, a fifty year old records clerk at LFPD and wife of Carl Lofton a.k.a., Thanatos. Mr. Lofton, fifty-two, was a project manager at Chris and Bean Inc., a software development firm located in downtown La Flore. Resentment, anger and frustration came to a head when the firm lost its city contract and Mr. Lofton was released due to budget cuts. Lashing out, he created Thanatos, and the hailstorm of fear, political upheaval and countless police hours hunting a killer that didn't exist. Mr. Lofton has been charged with felony public disorder and obstruction of justice. If convicted, he could serve four to six years in prison.

Special Agent Raymond Mack led the spirited and some believed, uncompromising charge on the Thanatos case. According to reports, he profiled Thanatos to the letter, but failed to profile the actual killer. We've tried to contact the special agent several times but he could not be reached. Something tells me, he's got some explaining to do.

Our heroine is a local detective who is no stranger to the media. Detective Tara Tanner was demonized by many in the tragic Sexton case a few years ago. Now, she's in the spotlight again and this time...she's being praised.

Taking on her first serial killer, the detective somehow managed to crack the killer's code. In an interview, she says she received a tip from a very reliable source that must remain anonymous. Well, to that very reliable source, the city of La Flore thanks you.

Detective Tanner was in pursuit of Daniel Wade when Detectives Cummins and McVey tracked down and apprehended Mr. Lofton late that Thursday afternoon for questioning. An hour later, they had a full confession, but that was not enough. There had been a few cases of false Thanatos confessions, so this time they needed more proof. Hours later, that proof came in the form of an incriminating email Mr. Lofton had sent to a colleague just two days before releasing the Thanatos letter. Mr. Lofton was off the hook, at least as the killer. A short time later, LFPD's Commander receive a call from the precinct's Background and Intelligence Division and heard this emotional and moving recording:

"*Agent Jenkins, this is Detective Tanner. I am at the Sleater Thomas Industrial Park at building number 1025 in pursuit of secondary suspect Daniel Wade. Suspect has a hostage and believed next victim. Hostage is a blond female in her late twenties. Suspect and hostage are inside the building. Suspect is believed to be armed and dangerous and the hostage is believed to be under duress. I am about to enter the building and pursue. I don't know why I called you but you've always come through for me. Maybe you can come through for me now, Agent Jenkins, thanks girlfriend, for everything*"

The Commander, realizing the message was sent nearly four hours earlier, quickly mobilized an armada of SWAT, choppers and patrol cars that converged on the abandoned site. Like a good old fashion western, the Cavalry arrived just in time as Detective Tanner was holding her own against a dangerous killer. When they saw a clear shot, they took out Mr. Wade and ended La Flore's deadly plague for good. Whatever martial arts the detective used to fend off such a dangerous predator…she must be a master at it.

Because of her heroism, Detective Tanner is to receive her second Medal of Valor, the only female to do so. The city of La Flore congratulates her on a job well done.

In our next segment, how solving this case helped Mayor Hondo Saks pull off a stunning come from behind victory in the most heated mayoral race in La Flore's history. On our next follow-up edition, it's now known as La Flore's sex scandal of the decade, sparking torrid media frenzy here and abroad. Hoping to take the Mayor's office, a past adulterous relationship was discovered between the highly popular Mayoral Candidate Eddie Lamar and an infamous Night Matriarch. Don't miss "The Rise and Fall of Eddie Lamar" on our next follow-up edition.

***

Tara lounges on the sofa, occasionally shaking her head at the conclusion of an exposé she feels is a bit over the top.

"The way they depicted me, you'd think I'd have an invisible plane parked out back," she thinks, hitting the off switch on the remote.

Sara and Megan however, were completely taken by the show's portrayal of their mother.

"Mom, that was great!" Megan says excitedly. "I can't wait to go to school tomorrow!"

"Mom, Meg is right. That was great," Sara adds. "I am curious though, you're no martial artist. How did you fend off the guy all that time?"

"What makes you think I'm not a martial artist?" Tara asks in a serious voice. Sara responds with a dubious look. After a moment, "Ok, let's just say it was divine intervention and leave it at that, shall we?"

"Mom, I'm hungry," Megan says.

"Sara, can you take your sister to the kitchen and fix her something…please?"

"What, you can't wiggle your nose and make stuff appear?"

"Just do it, Sara," Tara says, not in the mood for her daughter's cynical humor.

The sisters head to the kitchen. As her older sister continues, Megan stops and turns around, facing her mother.

"Mom, who gave you the tip?" she asks.

"Why do you ask?"

"I feel I may know this person."

Tara looks at her daughter for a moment.

"I'm sorry Meg. I can't disclose this person's name."

Tara can see a hint of disappointment in her daughter's face.

"I will tell you this," her voice perks at the prospect of what she is about to say, "You will definitely learn a lot more about this person as you get older...I promise."

Megan puckers her lip accompanied with shallow nods of her head. Tara can see the eleven year old is not completely satisfied with her response. She does not realize her mother has merely planted the seed that will assuredly one day come to fruition.

"OK, Mom," she responds.

"Could you do me a favor?"

"Why, sure, baby."

"Could you tell the person thank you for me, you know, for helping my mom?"

Her daughter's words strike an emotional cord catching Tara off guard. She freezes for a moment to get her composure, realizing her body just clearly gave away what her silence had concealed. Tara wonders whether her daughter's action was a sincere gesture or a deliberate and calculated scheme to read her body language. Either way...she was impressed.

"Yes, I will," she responds to her daughter's request. "As a matter of fact, it will be the first thing I do," she says with a big smile.

"Megan!" Sara scowls from the kitchen.

"I'm coming, I'm coming...Jeeze," she exclaims at her sister's calling.

She glances at her mother once more before turning around to go into the kitchen. As she walks away, a pleasant smile fills Tara's face. Just as her daughter is about to leave her sight,

"Thank you Meg," she says in a gracious and loving whisper.

A short time later, the phone rings. Viewing the caller ID, "Hey hun," Tara says.

"Hey there, Rock Star," Dale replies having watched the exposé with his partners from their firm. "That was some show, eh?"

Tara gives a sigh. "It was ok, I guess. Don't you think it was a little over the top?"

"Not at all. C'mon, Tara, you know they have to think about their ratings. Besides, if I were directing it, you would have had a ray gun and a cape."

"Great," Tara says unenthused.

"Are you still thinking about calling it quits?" Dale asks.

"I told the chief I'd let him know after my vacation."

"You know that decision's yours."

"It's as much yours as it is mine but thanks for putting it that way," she says.

"So today is your first training day in a while. It'll be good to see you at it again."

"Yeah, I can finally get consistent again. It's helped me more than you can imagine. When are you coming home?" Tara asks.

"Do I get an autograph?"

"You can get whatever you like," she says in her mother's seductive voice.

"I don't know what just happened," Dale says somewhat astounded, "But I like it. Are you sure you're up for that, this being your first day of training and all?"

"Oh, I think I can manage," she says, stretching out on the sofa. "The question is…are you?"

"Expect me home early tonight!"

They hang up. Tara takes a moment to reflect while lounging on the sofa with her feet up, and a peaceful expression on her face. The sun beams brightly through the large den window, making the room appear radiant. The moment makes Tara feel the city of La Flore, as well as her life, is finally getting back to normal. She looks over and sees Sara's latest tabloid edition.

"Oh boy," she says with amusement upon reading the headline. "My Personal Trainer Is a Space Alien And I Am Having His Baby." Tara is not a reader of tabloids, occasionally teasing Sara for the fetish but finds the headline too hard to resist. She picks up the paper and casually thumbs through its pages.

"Let me see. Miracle Pill That Makes Any Woman a 10," she reads aloud.

"So that's the Matriarch's secret," she asserts with a giggle.

As Tara continues to skim through the tabloid, she stumbles across a small piece with its title circled in red marker, tucked away at the bottom corner of a page. As she begins to read, her pleasant look slowly disappears and the humor she enjoyed evaporates. She looks around as an eerie darkness from passing clouds engulfs the room. Tara now wears a more serious expression as she's enthralled by the piece titled, "Former Green Beret Goes on Killing Spree". In the piece, the Green Beret claims a military Super Drug was administered to him years ago. As a result, he now experiences hallucinations and a split personality. The piece goes on to tell of a major cover up at the Pentagon and that two reporters covering the story have gone missing.

"Let me guess, this former Green Beret had no criminal record other than a couple of traffic violations," she says, repeating the words she used during Daniel's background check. She thinks of Randy Cox, his similar history and tragic end by his own hands.

All three of these guys were in Special Forces, she thinks.

"A Jekyll and Hyde drug," Tara says. She closes the paper, placing it in her lap.

Her desperate words chime in her head in a final attempt to reach Daniel before he slipped into his dark fantasy. *What happened to you at SEAL School?*

She recalls the look in Daniel's eyes during his final moments. She is convinced his intention was not to kill her, but to free himself the surest way he knew how. Tara looks around as the room brightens again. The clouds have moved on. Keenly focused on what she'd just read and her thoughts on Daniel, Tara responds to the interesting piece, "Hmm…"

She opens the paper once more and returns to the piece now focused on the next element she finds just as troubling, the bright red marker encircling the title. Tara knows this can mean a number of things. She also knows how carelessly audacious Sara can be when she sets her sights on something. She reads again how two reporters covering the story have gone missing.

"Sara," she sighs at the hint of what her daughter may be up to.

The sisters emerge from the kitchen. Megan, eager to text her friends, bolts upstairs.

"Don't run up the stairs Meg," Tara shouts, glad that Megan's leaving will allow her to spend time alone with Sara.

"Hey Mom, I have to go," Sara says, gathering her things. "I thought it was a great exposé and I'm really proud of you."

As she looks for something in particular, Sara stops when she finds it in the hands of her mother. Tara sees her daughter quickly add two and two together upon seeing her holding the tabloid paper with that all too familiar look. Tara, now confident that Sara knows why she has that look, weighs in.

"What's the meaning of this?" she calmly asks, displaying the tabloid piece to her daughter.

"Mom," Sara says in a manner conveying that her mother is overreacting.

"I came across that piece and found it interesting and circled the title because it made me think of your case; that's all," she says, slightly offended.

"What? Do you think with my abundant lack of experience as a reporter and the knowledge that two reporters with a hell of a lot more experience than me are missing, that I would even consider pursuing this story? Do you really think that Mom? I want to be as good a reporter as you are a detective. I also want to live to talk about it."

"Look me in the eyes and tell me you are not going to pursue this story."

"Mom, I'm not going to pursue this story."

"Period." Tara adds.

"Period...You didn't say period," Sara snaps.

"Well, I'm saying it now," Tara responds assertively.

"Ok. Period. Look, I really have to go."

She approaches her mother and delicately reaches out with an open hand to retrieve her tabloid paper. Tara stands to the exact height of her daughter and relinquishes the paper in a gingerly hand-over.

"I'm sorry if I've misjudged you. I really am," Tara says. She sees her daughter wants to keep matters as civil as does she. Mother and daughter engage in an embrace that, like on many past occasions, was more symbolic of a truce than actual affection.

"I'll walk you to the door."

They share some kind parting words before Sara exits and walks into the late afternoon sun. Tara watches her daughter from the living room window walk to her gold early model Honda civic. After a short crank of the engine, Sara's Honda comes to life. Tara smiles as she acknowledges her daughter's glance. She gives a gentle wave good bye and her daughter reciprocates.

"Love you," could be read from Sara's lips.

She backs out of the driveway and onto the vacant street before driving into the unknown. Tara stays at the window as Sara's Honda finally vanishes.

She looks over at the large wall clock to see it is time to head to her training appointment.

A short time later, Tara exits her front door and heads to her car. After tossing her gym bag in the back seat, she is startled to see her next-door neighbor, Faye Woodard, standing in her driveway, staring at her. Tara looks into a face harboring mixed feelings about Daniel, and about her. He changed Faye's life and Tara knows she thought the world of him. Tara is at a loss for words. She knows all too well the deep attachment some clients can have for their trainer, despite them being a serial murderer. After a moment, Tara watches

Faye get in her car and drive off, without uttering a word.

Nearly an hour passes before she enters the state of the art studio that looks much larger than its modest appearance from the outside. As Tara strolls on the treadmill, "Hmm, in rare form again," she says, hearing the bedlam from the training floor. Shortly afterward, a tall lean silver haired man emerges from the floor, drenched in sweat and face beet red.

"I got my fix for the day. Now it's your turn," he says in a rough voice.

"I guess it is," she says, watching the man exit the studio.

Moments later, "Hey, Tara."

The voice she hears is not Sasha's, a trainer she still holds in high regard, but it is the voice she feels that in her darkest hour, saved her life.

"Welcome back," Frank says, flashing a brilliant smile on his handsome face.

Tara, strolling nonchalantly on the treadmill, responds to Frank's words, with her mother's grin.

"Are you sure about this?" he asks of her leaving a great trainer to return to him.

Tara stops the treadmill. She casually steps off and faces her trainer. Looking into his face with eyes dark and piercing, she says with an air of confidence, "I've never been surer."

Acknowledgments

I cannot take sole credit for Fit to Kill. I would like to thank my fellow authors at the Olympia writer's group for keeping me focused, and Barnett Totskey in particular, for his insightful and brutal honesty. Tracy Papachristodoulou, I owe you big time, and I cannot thank Teresa Miller and Lenore Ingram enough. I must give a special thanks to Rhonda M. Huynh's efforts for making a great book cover. I would like to thank all of the folks who inspired many of the characters in Fit to Kill. Lastly, I thank my wife Diane, whose name always comes up in moments like these.

About the Author

Donnie Whetstone lives in Olympia, Washington. He has over twenty years of experience as a personal trainer and nutritional consultant. Donnie co-owns Fit Stop 24 Fitness Centers and is a national level competitive bodybuilder, looking to achieve a live long dream of attaining professional status. He's written several articles on fitness, training and nutrition and has a nonfiction training book in the works. He's currently working on a vampire novel titled Night Spear.